The Rider from Yonder

*Also by Norman A. Fox
in Thorndike Large Print®*

Reckoning at Rimbow
The Rawhide Years
Tall Man Riding
The Badlands Beyond
The Thirsty Land
Dead End Trail
Long Lightning
Silent in the Saddle
The Phantom Spur

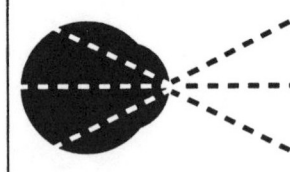
This Large Print Book carries the
Seal of Approval of N.A.V.H.

NORMAN A. FOX

The Rider from Yonder

Thorndike Press • Thorndike, Maine

Copyright, Norman A. Fox 1947; copyright renewed 1975 by Rosalea S. Fox.

All rights reserved.

First published in 1948.

Thorndike Large Print® Popular Series.

Published in 1993 by arrangement with Richard C. Fox.

The tree indicium is a trademark of Thorndike Press.

The text of this Large Print edition is unabridged.
Other aspects of the book may vary from the original.

Set in 16 pt. News Plantin by Barbara Ingerson.

Printed in the United States on acid-free, high opacity paper.∞

Library of Congress Cataloging in Publication Data

Fox, Norman A., 1911–1960.
    The rider from yonder / Norman Fox.
      p.   cm.
    ISBN 1-56054-711-1 (alk. paper : lg. print)
    1. Large type books. I. Title.
[PS3511.O968R5   1993]
813'.54—dc20   93-34585

TO
GRANDMA CAULFIELD
Affectionately . . .

at the edge of the boardwalk. Perching himself upon the hitch-rail, Melody took the guitar from his back, cuddled it, plucked a chord and began singing a song of his own composition:

"I know a gal on Chowder Crick,
Sassy as a squirrel and fatter'n a tick,
Hi, yo, diddle, di, day. . . .
Her teeth come out at the sunset hour,
Her complexion's the colour of a sack of flour,
One look from her and the cream goes sour,
Hi, yo, diddle, di, da-a-a-y. . . ."

This sample of his talents duly delivered to an unseen audience, he came down from the hitch-rail and strode into Jake's Eating Place. There was a long counter with stools, a scattering of tables, a half a dozen silent customers, an uncountable number of flies, and a greasy odour of frying steak.

Jake, himself, was behind the counter. A big man, Jake, with pendulous, underslung jaw, he had a greasy look as though long years of cooking had given him the characteristics of his own food. Melody, picking him as the boss of the establishment, favoured Jake with a smile and said, "What's on the bill of fare to-day?"

Chapter I
The Coming of Melody

When Stanton City saw him first, Melody Malone looked like any other saddle tramp except that he rode in with a silver-plated guitar slung across his back and a one-eyed, yellow tom-cat perched upon his shoulder. That would have made him a spectacle in any man's town. But as he came along the dusty, rutted main street, smiling at the eternal optimism of those who had dubbed this sorry collection of false fronts a city, there was scarcely a soul in sight. Marking this phenomenon with the casual thoroughness of a man used to giving attention to small details, he would have shrugged the matter aside, but he felt the sting of the cat's claws the moment he started the gesture. Plainly, Stanton City had something on its mind to-day.

There were eyes a-plenty marking Melody's entry, and he shortly became aware of them. There were men peering from every window and from the cover of doors held open a careful half-inch, and Melody's smile changed to a frown, for he began to feel like some stuffed museum piece. A man with a conscience less clear might have worried; a man with a soul more inhibited would have coloured with self-consciousness. Melody remained immune. Halting his horse before a livery stable, he came so carefully down from the saddle that the cat was able to maintain its precarious perch. To the hostler who was keeping cautiously within the shadow of the wide doorway, Melody said, "I want my horse grained." The hostler said, "Where did you pick up Brutus?"

"Brutus — ?" Melody took the cat from his shoulder, held him in his arms and gently knuckled the soft hollow beneath the cat's chin. "Found him loping across the prairie, about three miles out," Melody explained. "He was headed for town, and so was I, so I gave him a lift. He didn't mention his name. Somebody here own him?"

"Cats aren't owned by people," the hostler said, thereby revealing wisdom that was surprising in one so vacuous of face. "It's the other way around. Brutus, you might say, owns Stanton City. Every garbage barrel in town is his. But he fancies fish. Never saw a cat so concerned set on fish."

Melody lowered the huge beast to the ground, and Brutus, arching his back, leaned slantwise against Melody's leg, finished out a circle, and, with no more thank you than that, went walking away. There must have been some Persian in the ancestry of Brutus, for it was Melody's thought that from behind Brutus looked not unlike a plumed sheep. The hostler had made no move meanwhile, so Melody said pointedly, "My horse —"

"Sure," said the hostler and ran his eye up Melody's lanky length from his scuffed boots to his Levis which many tubbings had turned to the colour of skimmed milk, and up to a battered sombrero which looked like it had been slept on. The walnut-handled forty-five eased at Melody's hip held the hostler's passing attention, but his eyes dwelt the longest on Melody's face. It was a thin face, sun-browned, and high-boned as a Sioux's and handsome except that the nose was a trifle too long and the mouth a trifle too wide. A good face, it might have been worth credit with the hostler if Melody's garb hadn't marked him. The hostler said, "The freight is one dollar, stranger. Cash in advance."

Melody produced the dollar with no rancour, but the feat required considerable effort; for the dollar came in small pieces. While the hostler was counting these, Melody said,

"What ails this town? You'd think I was a plague when I rode in."

" 'Tain't you," the hostler said, his mind mostly on his arithmetic. "It's Breed Lenoir. Whenever he's on a spree, folks keep indoors. We get a day like this about once a month."

Now Melody might have asked further details concerning Mr. Breed Lenoir, and, had he done so, he would have learned that Lenoir was the employee of Quirt Hardin, whose Curling Quirt ranch was among the largest in this hill-hemmed stretch of grassland. Also, he would have been informed that it was Breed Lenoir's custom to come to Stanton City periodically for the purpose of putting himself outside as much drinking whisky as his gargantuan capacity allowed, and that on such occasions considerable violence ensued. Lenoir, liquored, showed a decided penchant for destruction and a marked talent for making himself a dangerous nuisance. Thus Stanton City had learned through bitter experience that it was wiser to keep itself scarce when Lenoir was on a rampage.

All this information would have been Melody's by the mere asking of a question, and thus his destiny in Stanton City might have taken a different turn. But he didn't ask the question. He had proposed to tarry here only long enough to take care of certain inward needs of himself and his horse, and half that task was as good as performed. He had learned that it wasn't his own appearance on the street that had sent the populace scurrying to cover, and with that his interest turned to more pertinent things. "Which is the largest restaurant?" he asked.

"Never measured 'em," said the hostler. "But Jake's Eating Place probably has the high tally on tables. You'll find it yonder."

Melody looked through the open doorway in the indicated direction, lifted his battered sombrero and combed his thick brown thatch with a lean brown hand, and then, setting the hat at a go-to-hell angle, he cut obliquely across the street, the guitar bouncing against his back. Stanton City was still gripped in its self-elected somnolence; the only sound came from the direction of the railroad depot where a train chuffed indolently in a siding, and Melody had the sensation of treading the street of a ghost town. His mind flitted briefly to Breed Lenoir, and he wondered what manner of man this ogre was and where the obnoxious Lenoir was keeping himself, and then he reached Jake's Eating Place.

The restaurant, a frame, unpainted building, had a wide frontage and an expanse of plate-glass window which could have stood a washing, and there was a gnawed hitch-rail

Jake's appraisal was quicker than the hostler's had been, but he apparently arrived at the same obvious conclusion. "We've got a dollar dinner," he said, "that's calculated to put fat on your ribs. You got the dollar, stranger?"

"Why, no," said Melody. "I did have, but I gave it to the hostler."

Jake's professional affability gave way to a quick truculence. "Do you think I feed every saddle bum who pokes his head in here?" he demanded.

Melody frowned but made no other show of temper than that. Turning his guitar over in his hands, he said, "Reckon you've got me pegged wrong, mister. I'm no tramp. Fact is, I'm a member of an old and honoured profession which has always paid its way. I'm a troubadour."

"A what — ?"

"A troubadour. I'm willing to sing for my supper. That lick and a promise I gave outside was for free. There's forty-eight more verses about that gal from Chowder Crick, and before I'm half through 'em, I'll likely have thought up a couple more."

Now Jake was one of those souls possessed of a sense of humour that was a great pride to him and a great pain to his associates. His customers' eyes were upon him — they were a scattering of cowhands, townspeople, and a drummer or two who was passing through — and Jake saw here a challenge to his own nimbleness of wit. So, crinkling his face into a caricature of a smile, Jake said, "You mean you want to swap a song for a free meal?"

"Some of your tables are empty," Melody pointed out. "Music will fetch you customers."

"Now that's a fair enough bargain," said Jake. "Mighty fair. But you could get yourself a free lunch over at the Elkshead Saloon and save your tonsils for another time."

Melody grimaced. "I couldn't even buy a glass of beer," he admitted. "The apron would run me out of the place if I ate without wetting my throat first."

"That's where you're mistaken, stranger," Jake countered. "The Elkshead isn't fussy that way. Tell you what, I'll give you my personal word of honour — and back it up with a free meal if I'm wrong — that if you'll head over to the Elkshead right now, the management won't say a word if you eat everything in sight. Hurry along and try it. And if you're hungry again, come nightfall, drop back here. Maybe we'll do business on that song-for-a-supper proposition."

Melody shrugged. "I'll take a whirl at this Elkshead Saloon," he said, and he parted the screen doors and was gone from the restaurant. Jake waited until the worn bootheels had ceased beating upon the boardwalk before he broke into uproarious laughter.

But his customers weren't sharing his mirth. One came to an abrupt stand — a tall, clean-shaven, middle-aged man who was so thin his black broadcloth suit and white waistcoat made him look like a dressed up tooth-pick. Glowering at Jake as he paid for his meal, this thin man said, "Jake, once I went to a funeral in Louisiana. They were having the last rites of a fine old man who'd made many friends. The minister preached a fine service, and the choir was never better, but when we all filed up to have our last look in the casket, we discovered that the undertaker had made a horrible mistake. He'd wheeled in a corpse whose funeral was scheduled for the same time the next day, and in that casket was the biggest, blackest, deadest Negro I'd ever seen. Looking back now, that mix-up had its funny side. But it wasn't funny at the time. Not a soul in that funeral hall laughed. But if you'd been there, Jake, you'd have howled!"

Jake was holding his sides. "Did that really happen, Mr. Floren?" he gasped. "They sent the wrong corpse over by mistake! A big, black, dead Negro! Wow!"

Otis Floren, Stanton's pioneer lawyer,

frowned. "Some things aren't laughing matters, Jake. You've just sent that stranger to the Elkshead. Naturally the management won't say a word to him, just as you promised. You know very well that the management cleared out of the saloon and is hiding until Breed Lenoir rides from town. And you know that Breed is over there holding down the place all by his lonesome and drinking himself to a pitch for murder, and ripe, probably, to shoot at anything that shows on the other side of the batwings!"

"Didn't tell him a single lie," Jake argued. "All I said was that the stranger would have no trouble from the management. Besides, that fellow was packing a gun as well as a guitar. If he rids the town of Lenoir for us, you'll all be thanking me."

"Usually I don't interfere with another man's horse-play," Otis Floren said. "Even when it gets to the point of being dangerous. But I shouldn't have let that stranger walk out of here without warning him about Breed. And I'm going straight to Sheriff Crain now and tell him what's up. Maybe he'll get over to the Elkshead before the stranger is killed."

"Anse Crain left town a couple hours ago," Jake said. "Just about the time Breed chased everybody out of the saloon. I'd guess that Anse headed to the Curling Quirt to fetch

Quirt Hardin into town. Quirt's the only man who can handle Breed Lenoir when Breed's got a skinful."

Otis Floren turned slightly pale. He was a man who'd watched a frontier grow and who had coped with violence with a row of law books, but in no other way. Within him lofty principles had often warred with a weaker flesh, and there was such a struggle going on now. He looked through the unwashed window and tried to catch a glimpse of Melody Malone, but Melody had vanished, and the Elkshead wasn't visible from here. He took a step towards the door, but hesitation was in it. And just then three riders came thundering along the street and wheeled to a dust-boiling stop at the hitch-rail before the high building that housed Floren's office.

"Sam Weaver, Rocky Lynch, and Dallas Spade have just ridden in," Jake said unnecessarily. "Better not keep 'em waiting, Mr. Floren. Town talk says the bunch of you are holding a meeting this afternoon to figger out a way to bust the scheme that Quirt Hardin figgered out to hog-tie you."

"Yes," Floren muttered absently, his brow suddenly furrowed with a new worry. "The scheme...." He went out through the screen doors and stood for a moment on the sidewalk. No sign of Melody Malone, but Floren, peering hard and wishing he wore his glasses, thought that the swinging doors of the Elkshead were still swaying slightly, as though a man might have just pushed them inward.

Still the lawyer hesitated, principle warring with the flesh once again, and he looked around him like a man trying to borrow courage, but there was no one to borrow it from. Not in Stanton City to-day. He said, "The scheme. . . ." as though trying to force his mind to another and more practical duty, and then he went out into the dust of the street, not towards the Elkshead and the succour that Melody Malone might be sorely needing, but towards his own office and the group who would be waiting him there.

Chapter II
Quirt Hardin's Way

The scheme that had fetched five people to a rendezvous in Otis Floren's office was one that had required a natural talent for rapacity, a patience almost Mephistophelean, and a boldness that would be like a brandished club now that the hour was ripe. Also, it contained an element of chance. The spider, having spun his web, may snare the flies — or he may snare disaster. The scheme had taken an agile mind at its inception, a quick hand during the developing, and it would require a ruthless fist before the game was finished. All these belonged to Quirt Hardin; that was the way he worked.

And that was why the three men who sat in creaking, uneasy chairs in Floren's office over the mercantile store were a tight-lipped trio as they watched Floren pace the room nervously, his hands clasped beneath the long tails of his coat. The girl alone held to serenity.

She was tall and compactly built; and a blue, tailored suit and the prim way in which her brown hair was piled high upon her head gave her a touch of austerity that blinded a man at first look to the fact that she was beautiful. She sat with her hands placidly folded over a reticule in her lap, saying nothing, just waiting.

Rocky Lynch broke the silence. He was the biggest of the three who'd just ridden in, a huge, blocky man with an iron-grey moustache and a red-veined face which indicated an explosive temper that had never known a tight rein. He said, "Floren, you've got bad news written all over your face, by gar. We didn't ride to town to watch you wear out your carpet. Spill it, and get it over with!"

Floren ceased his pacing and ran his eyes restlessly round his office. It was a big room, its walls lined with the cases containing his precious law books, and there was a desk in the centre, and the scattering of chairs upon which the four were seated. Floren contemplated a brass spittoon beside the desk, reached instinctively for a tobacco plug which was the one vice he permitted himself, glanced at the girl who gave no nod of approval, and carefully stowed the plug back in his pocket. Clearing his throat, Floren said, "Miss Corday has been in town two weeks now, and I've given her some inkling of the situation. But before we proceed, I'd better present her with all the facts."

Rocky Lynch snorted. "Do you always beat around the bush, Floren? Is she Chance Corday's heir, or ain't she?"

Floren looked exceedingly uncomfortable. "She's mentioned in his will, of course. She's his niece, and his only living relative so far as he knew. There are certain facts which I am not yet at liberty to divulge. But she'll be living in the C-C Connected ranch-house as soon as it is rebuilt, and that means she'll be vitally concerned in this matter which has brought us together."

Dallas Spade, from the chair nearest Anita Corday's, said, "The boys are coming along fine with their work on the house, Miss Corday. You'll be able to move out of the hotel mighty soon."

He was the youngest man in the room, this Spade — young enough to have taken that second look at Anita Corday and seen what the others had missed. And it would have been noticeable to the observant that Spade wore his best silk shirt to-day and that his lean, handsome face was shaved until it shone, and that his silky, yellow hair had been given a good deal of attention. Foreman of the mammoth C-C Connected, he was a good hand with cows and bright enough to hold his position against the aspirations of older men. Anita Corday thanked him with a smile.

The third man, Sam Weaver, lay sprawled in his chair; a lean fellow, all arms and legs, he had a good-humoured face and a certain warmth that made him a popular man at dances and box socials. Middle-aged and book-learned, he had a natural flair for gallantry, and he said now, "You're still welcome to move out to our Anvil ranch until the C-C house is ready for you, Miss. My wife would be happy to have you."

"Thank you," Anita said. "If Mr. Spade runs into any unexpected delays, I'll remember your offer. But the hotel has been quite comfortable. Until to-day. Now everybody is keeping their doors bolted because some drunken half-breed is supposed to start terrorising the town."

Floren, thus reminded of Breed Lenoir and a man who might be needing help, winced. "Miss Corday," he said, clearing his throat again, "I've asked you to be at this meeting to hear something that is vital to all the ranchers whose acreage lies far to the south of here. Your uncle's C-C Connected is one of those spreads. Sam Weaver's Anvil is another. So is Rocky Lynch's Lazy-L. Those three ranches lie side by side, and two, the C-C and the Lazy-L, abut upon the Curling Quirt which is to the north and between them and town."

Anita nodded. "I think I've got the picture."

"This stretch of range is known as the Cinnibar," Floren went on. "So-called for the hills that hem it on all sides. The range is roughly oval-shaped, and the hills pinch together at the southern end, forming a pass which is the back door of the country, an opening known as the Pass of the Blackrobes, since it was first discovered by Jesuit missionaries in the early days. It's wild tangled country to the south, good for winter pasturage, perhaps, but hardly terrain over which to trail cattle."

Again Anita nodded. "The pattern is becoming clear. You've hinted at the problem before. I was ranch-raised, Mr. Floren. In Wyoming. And I've been teaching school these past three years in a little cow-town in southern Idaho. The country I'm used to is a bit different than that around here, but I see the situation, I believe. The problem of the ranchers to the south, men such as my uncle was, is to get their cattle to market."

"Precisely," Floren said. "Except that heretofore there has never been a problem. The railroad goes through here, and you've doubtless seen the loading pens. The ranchers had only to make their fall roundups, trail their cattle north to town, load them into stock cars and ship them off to Eastern markets. But now there's a new factor to be considered."

"Get at it!" Rocky Lynch urged. "Tell her about the strip. Tell her what Quirt Hardin's gone and done!"

Floren frowned. "I'm getting to that. You see, Miss, most of the local ranchers are the sons or grandsons of Texas people, men who trailed herds northward when Texas graze grew thin from overstocking, and who settled in this virgin country. Those men brought in the long-horn, weathered the Montana blizzards, fought Indians and rustlers, and eventually developed a better brand of beef. Then the Homestead Act encouraged the coming of sodbusters, and the cattlemen woke up to the fact that they had no legal claim to the land they'd pre-empted and called their own. Some ignored the law and held the sodbuster off with a gun. Some bowed to the inevitable and took steps to repair their legal standing. They filed on one hundred and sixty acres for themselves and had their cowboys file on adjacent acreage and then paid their cowboys for this service once title was established. That way the ranchers became legal possessors. All three ranches represented here to-day were legalised in this manner."

"Then what is the problem?" Anita asked. "I'd supposed that you were preparing to explain that this Quirt Hardin fellow had managed somehow to lay claim to his neighbours acreage."

"It's worse than that!" Rocky Lynch snorted before Floren could get in his say. The lawyer's eyes beseeched silence.

"The original surveys which established homestead boundaries were not above challenge," Floren said. "A lot of those surveys were made from hotel windows — the surveyors having a good time at government expense and turning in reports that were largely guesswork. But nobody ever had occasion to challenge any Cinnibar survey. There were no disputes, nothing to gain by it. Some months ago, though, Quirt Hardin brought in professional surveyors and had them look over the range. Quirt explained that he had some fencing in mind and just wanted to make sure where the proper lines ran before he put up barbed wire. None of us thought a great deal about it. If there'd been a water-hole in question, or some prize acreage at stake, we might have been more curious. As it was, the surveyors came and went without much heed being paid to them."

"And now —"

"And now it has developed that the old lines

were indeed wrong. In fact there is quite a wide strip running east and west the entire width of the Cinnibar range — a strip belonging to nobody because nobody had actually, filed upon it. Previously established homesteads had lapped over on to it without realising that there was no legal right to do so."

Anita said, "Are you getting around to telling me that Quirt Hardin has filed on this strip?"

Floren shook his head. "That land is no longer available for homesteading. It belongs to the government and can be leased for grazing purposes. Quirt Hardin had leased it, and is fencing it off. Which is now his legal right. It is also his right to see that it is not trespassed upon. Now do I make the situation clear!"

Anita Corday still had a question in her eyes, and that was because the human element was the unknown equation to her, but Dallas Spade supplied the missing factor. He said, very quietly, "What he means is that Quirt Hardin can stop our herds from crossing that strip when we head to town to ship our cattle off to market. He can collect toll, if he wishes, for placing a gate and allowing us passage. Most men, having leased grazing land, would permit their neighbours to use a lane for their own needs. The thing we're afraid of is that

Quirt Hardin's scheme from the first was to put us legally at his mercy. Your uncle was the only man to suspect that. He spoke his fears before he died."

Rocky Lynch said, "And that brings the rest of us right back to where we were when we walked into this room. Now do some real talking, Floren. You said you'd look up the law. Can Hardin get away with this!"

Floren gestured futilely to a dozen law books spread open upon his desk.

"He can," he said simply.

Lynch started out of his chair. "Then what in blazes did you fetch us here for? You could have sent us that word without bringing us to town!"

Floren coughed. "I'm the legal adviser to all three ranches," he said. "I've looked up the law for you, and the law is of no help. The government presumes that Hardin leased the land for the usual purposes. There is the law of custom, of course, a loophole which decrees that anything that is established custom on a range becomes a binding law as effecting that range. But we can't hale Hardin into court and prove by precedent that under such circumstances Cinnibar ranchers would allow their neighbours passage across The Strip. There is no precedent. No, I've failed you as a lawyer. I've brought you together to-day in the hopes that in union there'd be strength. The same problem faces the three southern ranches. We've got to solve it together."

Sam Weaver unravelled his long legs and said, "Got any ideas, Otis?"

Outside, hooves thundered along the street, the sound loud and compelling in the hush that claimed the town. Otis Floren turned to the window looking down upon the street, and he said, "Talk about the devil — Quirt Hardin and that gunman of his, McTeague, have just ridden in. But likely they've come at Sheriff Crain's request. I heard that Crain went to get Quirt to handle Breed Lenoir."

Sam Weaver said again, patiently, "Any ideas, Otis? About how we're to handle the strip situation?"

Floren said wearily, "I was hoping you gentlemen would have the ideas."

"I argue that patience and tact will get us further than anything else," Weaver said. "When Hardin asks toll, let's try to argue him into lowering his toll. We can always hint that we'll head our cattle south through the pass if we're forced to it. That would mean we'd work the tallow off them and take three times as long getting to the railroad, but Hardin will likely be willing to compromise if he thinks we mean it."

"And if he calls our bluff — ?" Dallas Spade asked.

"Then we'll head them south."

Rocky Lynch's red face had turned redder with angry thought. "I say let's give him a fight! He'll have a lot of fencing to do to close off The Strip, and he can't patrol all that fence night and day. As fast as he strings wire, we'll cut it."

Floren quickened with interest. "It's pretty important that I know exactly what you mean, Rocky," he said intently. "Are you proposing to cut wire by night? Or do you mean to defy Hardin openly and take the consequences?"

Lynch spluttered incoherently and had a time finding words. "Wa-al, I didn't exactly mean to go right out and ask for a fight. Not yet, anyway. I guess it's pretty plain to all of us now why Hardin imported a gunman like this McTeague and has the fellow sticking closer to him than a shadow. But I didn't like the idea of taking this lying down."

"I see," Floren said and nodded as though the question and answer had had a deep significance to him. "Miss Corday? I suppose, at least at present, that it's up to you to speak for the C-C Connected. We'd like to hear what you have to say."

"It won't be much," Anita said. "After all, I was practically a stranger to my uncle.

Doubtless any one of you, was far better acquainted with Chauncey Corday and —"

"*Chauncey!*" Lynch interjected. "Was Chance Corday's real name Chauncey? I always reckoned he was called Chance because he was the chanciest gent in ten counties."

Three pairs of eyes frowned him to silence, and Anita said, "The point I'm trying to make is this: if the destiny of the C-C Connected is to be in my hands — and I gather from what you've admitted to me, Mr. Floren, that it will be, at least for the present — then I want to proceed as my uncle would have proceeded. But one of you will have to tell me what his choice would have been."

"I think I can do that," Dallas Spade began, and then his voice trailed away. Boots were clumping along the hall, beyond the door that gave into this room; there was no knock, but the door swung inward, and Quirt Hardin stood there.

"Howdy," he said and smiled. "Mind if I come in?" But he was moving inside as he spoke, and behind him strode his gunman, McTeague.

Up until this moment, Rocky Lynch had been the biggest man in the room in point of pounds, but Quirt Hardin was the biggest man on Cinnibar range. Fat hung on him in folds, bulging his clothes until it seemed that his buttons were in perpetual peril, ballooning his face so that his eyes were lost in an immensity of dross. About him there was opulence, made apparent by the expensive texture of his clothes and evidenced also by the pearl-inlaid handle of the forty-five at his hip, and he possessed as well a hearty joviality that screened the fact that no gesture of his, no word and no thought was ever wasted. A quirt dangled from a loop about his puffy right wrist; the quirt that had given him his sobriquet and suggested his brand.

He said, "McTeague and I just rode in. Stopped for a cup of coffee over at Jake's and heard that you folks were holding a palaver. Judged that it was about me. We reckoned there was no harm in our being in on it. Isn't that so, McTeague?"

McTeague merely nodded, and even the nod was lost upon Hardin, for McTeague still stood behind his master. Tall and lean, McTeague had never been seen in anything but funereal black, and his face was a mummy's face, sun-blackened and inscrutable as a rock. If his vocabulary had ten words to it, there were eight that Stanton City had yet to hear. So far he had been reported to have said yes and no on occasion — mostly no. He had come here with a reputation made in other parts, and he had let it do his talking for him. His gun was ivory-handled, and he wore it tied down.

These were the two who had entered, and their entry was so sudden and so unexpected as to leave the five speechless, but, surprisingly, it was Floren who recovered first, and Floren who made a display of courage now. He said, "You're not welcome here, Hardin. Nor your hired killer. This is a private discussion and not intended for your ears. I trust that's plain enough!"

Hardin had discovered Anita Corday, and his sombrero came off to reveal an expanse of shining baldness as he tipped in a bow that was astonishingly graceful for one of his girth. "Chance Corday's niece, I presume," he said. "I'd heard that you were in town. I hope you'll favour the Curling Quirt with a visit before long."

Dallas Spade coloured, and speech trembled on his lips, and McTeague suddenly moved one boot a half an inch ahead of the other. But Anita Corday staved off the potentialities of violence. She said, "I might be pleased to do that, Mr. Hardin, but how would I get across your fenced off strip to reach the Curling Quirt?"

Hardin laughed, a deep, booming laughter that rolled through the room and chased echoes out of the corners. "So you *have* been talking about The Strip," he said. "I thought so. You've learned what I've done, and you've anticipated my scheme, and now all of you are sitting around looking as though the sky had fallen. There's no cause for alarm, gentlemen. No cause at all. I'm putting in a gate for your convenience. And all I'm charging is one dollar a head for bringing your cattle through."

"A dollar a head — !" Lynch exploded. "Why, man alive — !"

Hardin spread his hands in a gesture beseeching tolerance. "Your fathers and grandfathers paid ten cents a head for clearance papers giving them the privilege of taking long-horns out of Texas in the old days. And they paid it knowing full well that many of those long-horns would die before they reached the northern markets or northern graze. You men are raising a superior beef, worth many times on the hoof what a long-horn fetched. Surely my fee isn't exorbitant."

"Look, Hardin," Sam Weaver said. "You know very well that will add up to thousands of dollars every season. Be reasonable."

"It's robbery," Lynch growled. "Plain robbery."

Hardin's smile grew expansive. "It's legal. I reckon that Floren, here, has already told you there's no loop-hole. Come, gentlemen.

I'm merely doing what any one of you would have done if he'd seen the opportunity first."

Dallas Spade said, "Don't be so cockeyed sure of that Hardin."

It was a challenge and an insult the way he said it, and it pierced through Hardin's show of affability and brought a high glint to his eyes, but before words came to him, the gun spoke. The sound was dimmed by distance and muffled by walls, but it reached all of them clearly enough, and Rocky Lynch said with accuracy, "A shotgun! Somebody's just fired a shotgun in one of the buildings on the street."

McTeague got across the room in a quick, gliding movement and was the first man to the window. He had a look outside, and something within his range of vision gave him his cue, for he summed up his instant conclusion in three terse words: "The Elkshead. Lenoir."

And that was when Otis Floren again remembered the stranger, Melody Malone, who had been tricked into entering the saloon where Breed Lenoir, drunk and ripe for murder, lurked. And even though the others didn't share Floren's knowledge, a dollar would have gotten any reasonable odds in that room at that minute that somebody had been readied for the undertaker when that shotgun had gone off.

Chapter III
Heir Unapparent

Melody Malone, angling across the street from Jake's Eating House to approach the Elkshead Saloon, was not in a state of such blissful ignorance as Jake had supposed. Not by a jugful. Horseplay was the West's own peculiar brand of humour, the lusty fun-making of a young and lusty land, and Melody could smell a joke a mile off when the wind was right. Jake had been a little too eager to get Melody to sample the Elkshead's free lunch, a little too lavish in his promise. All this had tolled a warning bell in Melody's consciousness.

But there is an old saying that you have to bite to learn, and the word bite had a special significance to Melody at the moment, for he hadn't tasted food since early morning. He anticipated an intolerant attitude on the part of the Elkshead's management, and this, he supposed, was the basis of Jake's joke. But there was always the hope that music might sooth even a saloon owner's savage breast. He didn't anticipate Breed Lenoir.

The Elkshead had a wide porch with a wooden awning above it, and Melody, mounting the three steps to the porch, became aware that the saloon was strangely silent. This gave him pause, but only for an instant. At this afternoon hour, the patronage would be skimpy, and, besides, this whole town seemed to be emulating Rip Van Winkle to-day. The only horse at the saloon's hitch-rail bore a Curling Quirt brand, but this carried no meaning to Melody. The livery stable man had mentioned Lenoir, but Melody hadn't probed for the further details that would have forewarned him now, and thus his destiny took him inexorably onward. He spread the batwings apart with a forward movement of his hands, stepped inside and blinked to adjust his eyes from the brilliance of the street to the semi-darkness of the interior, and something swished by his cheek and thunked into the batwings. From the corner of his eye Melody saw it — a long-bladed skinning knife, its handle still vibrating. This was his introduction to Breed Lenoir.

The Elkshead was a big saloon — Stanton City's biggest — and the bar-room was vast in its emptiness. Along one wall ran the bar, silent and deserted, and behind it was the largest mirror Melody had ever seen. The rest of the floor was given to tables and chairs for poker players. The only patron of the place was seated at one of these tables, a huge hulk of a man, greasy-skinned with stringy black hair showing beneath his sombrero. His garb was that of a working cowhand, but his sombrero was banded by silver conchas, and, in addition to a holstered forty-five, he wore a knife scabbard at his belt. The scabbard was empty. But as Melody raised his hand and wrenched the knife from the batwings, the big man also raised a hand to the nape of his neck, and another scabbard, sewed inside his shirt collar, and thus produced a second knife, a mate to the one that had greeted Melody.

"By gar," said Breed Lenoir. "You got knife. Me got knife. Now we fight, eh?"

He came lurching to a stand, spreading his legs apart and hunching his wide shoulders, and Melody saw that Lenoir was bigger than he first appeared and that all of him was muscled and wiry. Also, he saw murder in the fellow's sharp, black eyes. Not murder for gain, or murder for lust, or for any of the reasons that man reverts to Cain, but just plain murder. And, seeing this, Melody knew now why all Stanton City took to cover when Breed Lenoir came to town to do his liquoring.

And Lenoir was full of liquor. He'd transported quite an array of bottles from the bar to the table, and they covered the table top. Apparently he'd been sampling from various bottles, and those that hadn't suited his taste had been hurled at the bar railing, for there was a considerable scattering of broken glass at a spot not far from the table.

Now Lenoir shoved at the table with his free left hand, and sent it crashing over, and his lip peeled back to reveal a set of exceedingly white teeth. Outside, hooves thundered along the street — Rocky Lynch and Sam Weaver and Dallas Spade had just ridden in — but to Melody the sound seemed remote and belonging to another world. And now there was a great fear in Melody, and he was honest enough to recognise it — not the fear of one man for another, for this Breed Lenoir was not a man, but something crawled up out of a cave, something left over from an age where the claw and the fang ruled.

"Now, look —" Melody said placatingly.

"We fight!" insisted Breed Lenoir.

"With knives?" Melody said desperately and saw then the first faint shape of inspiration. "That's kid stuff. Let's play 'Split-Finger.'"

"Split-Feenger — ? What ees this Split-Feenger?"

"Nothing to it." Melody strode across to

the bar. "The early day trappers used to play the game on dull days. Lots of fun, if you've got the nerve." He placed one hand, palm down, on the bar's polished surface and held the knife six inches above it, the blade pointed downward. "The idea is for you to try and stick me before I can pull my hand away. If you miss, then I get a try at you. Loser buys a drink."

Lenoir's dark eyes glittered with suspicion. Patently this was not according to the usual programme. Always before Breed Lenoir had ridden into town, begun tanking up at the Elkshead, and, at a certain stage, proceeded to run the other patrons and the management out of the place. Thereafter it was his custom to drink in solitude, feeding his ego on the fact that no man dared poke his head within the place when Breed Lenoir was taking his pleasure. In due time this mood always changed to one of fancied insult. By gar, thees people theenk they are too good to drink with Breed Lenoir, eh? I theenk thees town she needs damn' good shooting up!

Whereupon Lenoir would emerge from the Elkshead to find an empty street, for Stanton City had learned through sad experience what to expect. His six-shooter uncased, Lenoir would do considerable damage to plate glass, nick any laggard he caught in the open, and eventually ride out, whooping and hollering as he went. Quirt Hardin would come to town, pay the damage at a figure set by himself, give Lenoir a slight admonishment and let it go at that; for Lenoir's very penchant for violence was to be part of Hardin's armament when the time was ripe. This was the monthly ritual, and the pattern never changed.

But to-day it had, and therefore Lenoir was puzzled — and suspicious. First of all, this stranger had dared to show his face in here. That had been an affront in itself, and the hurled knife had been the instinctive answer. That lust to kill had quickly flamed within Breed Lenoir, and he'd demanded a knife fight, but the stranger had countered with a proposal that they play Split-Finger. This Split-Finger business was a new one on Breed Lenoir, but it appealed to his bloodthirstiness, and there'd been a challenge to his courage wrapped up in the invitation. He crossed to the bar, lurching only slightly, for some men get drunk in the legs, but Lenoir got drunk only in the brain.

"Spread out your hand, m'sieu," Lenoir ordered.

Melody did so, his right hand this time, and he could feel his pulse pounding as Lenoir raised his knife aloft. This Lenoir was entirely too steady; Melody could hear the man's breathing and smell the reek of Lenoir's breath, but Melody was keeping his eyes on that blade. A shard of sunlight, slanting through the saloon's window, rippled on the steel, and then the blade was descending, descending with all the force of Lenoir's arm behind it. Melody didn't have to will himself to withdraw his hand. That was instinctive. The knife bit deeply into the planking, almost grazing the nail on Melody's longest finger, and the blade was embedded in the bar.

At that moment Melody exploded into action. Dropping his own knife, his right hand snatched at the gun in Lenoir's holster, and he plucked it free and sent it sailing away. His left hand closed around Lenoir's right wrist and Melody twisted, tearing Lenoir's fingers from the haft of the embedded knife, and he shoved Lenoir, sending the big man staggering away from the bar.

All this had been Melody's intent from the first. Once into the saloon and faced with the realisation that Jake's joke had been on the deadly side, he had needed a plan of operation. His instinct had been to turn and bolt through the batwings, but he couldn't travel faster than a bullet, and his exposed back would have been a temptation to Lenoir, who had had a second knife in his hand. Melody's need, then, had been to disarm

Lenoir, and this he had managed to do by arousing the man's interest in the game of Split-Finger. And now they were man to man, and Melody was quickly peeling the guitar from his back and sending it sliding along the bar; for Lenoir was coming at him with death flaming in his eyes, and a bobbing guitar might be a handicap in what was to follow.

Melody had been in a few fist fights in his time, but he couldn't remember ever having won one. There'd been a couple that had been mighty near a draw, but this was the first time Melody had ever fought with the realisation that he was fighting for his life. His gun still swung at his hip, but he had his own good reason for not touching it. The two came at each other as long-horns come at an unhorsed rider, and when they crashed together Melody's fists were flailing, and his barrage of blows sent Lenoir reeling backward. Some of the drunken confidence went out of Lenoir, but the murder was still in his eyes. He came back more cautiously, and they stood toe to toe, swapping hard, bone-jarring blows, fighting silently and with deadly intent.

Whisky had not robbed Lenoir of power, and it had whetted his natural ferocity, but his timing was not always accurate, and that was Melody's only advantage. He quickly saw Lenoir's strategy. Lenoir was trying to force him backward, and, by doing so, Lenoir hoped to get his hands on one of those knives. Therefore Melody kept the man constantly busy, refusing to retreat the while, and Lenoir soon adopted new tactics.

Falling back from a blow of Melody's and almost tripping over the bar rail, Lenoir righted himself by clutching at the bar, and kicked savagely at Melody. The man's boot swinging upward, Melody caught at it and twisted, and Lenoir went down, but Melody went down with him. Locked together, they rolled across the floor, in imminent danger from that scattering of broken glass; and Melody struggled to break Breed's hold. In rough and tumble fighting, Lenoir's huge bulk and wiry strength were an advantage, so Melody wrenched free and got to a stand, heaving and panting. Lenoir was instantly up, but the man darted away from Melody, ran the length of the bar and bobbed around it. Melody supposed he was after the embedded knife, so Melody darted to the knife, wrenched it free and flung it to the far corner. But Lenoir had bobbed from view, and now he jack-in-the-boxed into sight again, a sawed-off shotgun clutched in his hands and his lip peeled back in a grimace of triumph.

That shotgun was obviously the bartender's, kept handy to quell anything that approached a riot, and Lenoir, familiar with this saloon, had remembered it. At that moment Melody would have sold his chance of living for a Confederate shinplaster, but instinct sent him diving to the floor. Landing on his chest, he went skidding through the sawdust just as the shotgun roared, the sound thunderous, and buckshot whistled over Melody like the breath of death. Lenoir had let go with both barrels. Melody came to his feet, a red haze of anger swimming before him, and he saw Lenoir clambering over the bar, brandishing the shotgun like a club.

The trouble with a temper was that no matter how hard a man sat on it, there were times when it got away from him. This was one of those times. The fear was gone from Melody now, but so was all sense, all attention to strategy. He met Lenoir half-way, but he couldn't have told how he got the shotgun from Lenoir, but it, too, went sailing to a corner. They grappled against the bar, and Melody freed himself, spun Lenoir around with a blow that Melody felt all the way up to his elbow, and then Melody followed up with a haymaker that sent Lenoir staggering backward into the tables.

Melody was upon him as Lenoir went down, and, dragging the stunned man to his feet, Melody let him have an uppercut that took

Lenoir half-way to the batwings. So far this fight had been silent and deadly. Now it was noisy and deadly, the sound of splintering furniture had doubtless carried beyond the batwings. Men were shouting out yonder on the street; the whole town had likely heard the shotgun, but Melody had forgotten there was a town. Lenoir, tripping over his own feet, had gone down again, but Melody wrapped his hand in Lenoir's shirt-front and hauled the man erect. Lenoir tried weakly to raise a guard, but Melody's fist slashed through it again, and this blow sent Lenoir backward through the batwings and across the porch, and when Melody came plunging after him, Lenoir was whimpering in the dust of the street, sober and beaten and abject.

Melody saw the men coming running; he saw the group spilling out of Jake's Eating Place and from a dozen doorways, and he saw the little knot that was closing the distance between the mercantile store building and the Elkshead, the group that was headed by a puffing fat man and a granite-faced man in black with a tied-down gun. But Melody was oblivious to all of them. Again he wrapped his fist in Lenoir's shirt and hauled him to a stand. "Git riding, and git riding fast!" Melody snapped. "Don't let me ever see your face in these parts again!"

He sent Lenoir away from him with a shove that almost knocked the legs out from under the man, and Lenoir went lurching to the lone horse at the Elkshead's hitch-rail. He was pulling himself into the saddle when Quirt Hardin came to a puffing stop before the saloon. There was just wind enough left in Hardin to call out. "Breed! Come back here!"

But Breed Lenoir was deaf to his master's voice. Behind Hardin and McTeague were Otis Floren, Rocky Lynch, Sam Weaver, Dallas Spade, and Anita Corday, but Melody spoke only to the fat man. He said, "I told him to lope. He knows I mean it."

The anger was running out of him now, and he grinned, feeling a little foolish. He said, "I didn't mean him no harm, but he was real set on playing rough. Reckon this range will be better off without him."

Hardin measured Melody with a stare that searched for assets that hadn't interested the hostler or Jake when they'd made a like appraisal. And then Hardin said, "You sent him away, mister. Reckon you can call him back."

Lenoir had freed the tie-rope and wheeled his horse and was heading away from the group, but he was still within range of a lifted voice. Melody said, "I made all the say to him that I'm going to say."

The fat man's eyes widened, and it was

Melody's thought that Hardin looked for all the world like a man of a mind to trade in his ears for a new set; and the tall gent with the tied-down gun took a step forward that brought him from behind the fat man and to Hardin's side. Hardin said, "Stranger, are you defying me?" and Otis Floren was suddenly taking an intent interest in all this.

The question had already been answered, answered by action, or, rather, by Melody's refusal to take action. Breed Lenoir had lifted his horse to a gallop and was gone beyond recall, riding out with no whooping and hollering but with his head lowered and the spirit taken out of him. What might have happened then was to be a subject for cracker barrel speculation in long evenings to come, but what did happen was that Brutus entered the scene.

The tom-cat came from beneath the porch of the Elkshead, huge and tawny and considerably dishevelled, and started toward the group with an attitude that indicated an utter unconcern for the petty affairs of men. He came as an exiled king might have come, shabby and imperious, and Quirt Hardin spied him, and the colour went out of Hardin's face and he clawed for the gun he wore. He got the gun out of leather and got it raised, and the onlookers who'd expected that this was an action against the stranger were astonished to see the barrel jerk downward to catch Brutus in the sights. The gun roared, but just as it roared Melody was lunging forward. His arm struck at Hardin's, and bullet geysered dust; and Brutus was a yellow streak vanishing under the nearby porch.

"The cat," said Melody, "is a friend of mine."

Quirt Hardin merely looked at him, and then Hardin cased the gun he held in his hand, and in that instant Melody saw more murder in Hardin's eyes than he'd seen in Breed Lenoir's. Without a word, Hardin turned away, and McTeague, taking this cue from his master, followed after him, the two trudging off down the street. After that there was a full thirty seconds of silence, and Dallas Spade broke it by saying, "There's one thing I can't savvy, stranger. The sign says you and Breed mixed it up plenty, and a moment ago Quirt Hardin went for a gun. It must have looked to you like he was aiming on using it on *you*. All this time you've had a forty-five at your hip. Why haven't you used it?"

Melody grinned. "No bullets. Swapped them off in the last town to stable my horse."

Otis Floren had been like a man in a trance. Now the lawyer came to life again and cleared his throat. Melody was turning away, his intention being to get his guitar from the saloon, and Floren said, "Just a minute, please." Then he turned to the others. "Gentlemen, you've asked whether Miss Corday is the heir to the C-C Connected, and I was forced to give you evasive answers. You'll understand why when I explain more fully. But now I'm at liberty to tell you this much: this gentleman, this stranger in our midst, is the heir to Chance Corday's acreage."

That was the bombshell he dropped among them, and it stunned all of them beyond action, save two. Dallas Spade, as before, managed to find words, and he said, "You must be crazy, Floren! *Him!* Why, he's nothing but a saddle-bum, from the looks of him! You mean I'm taking *his* orders from here on out!"

The other person who hadn't been turned into stone by Floren's pronouncement was Melody himself. He'd vanished into the saloon after his precious guitar.

Chapter IV
The Will of Chance Corday

They were again gathered in Otis Floren's office over the mercantile store, the same four in the same creaking, uneasy chairs, and they sat in the same tight-lipped silence which had attended their awaiting Floren's word on the legality of Quirt Hardin's scheme. Anita Corday, her former aplomb shaken, fingered her reticule nervously; Dallas Spade frowned at a fly-specked law certificate upon the wall; Rocky Lynch's red-veined face was contorted with deep thinking. Of them all, only Sam Weaver remained reasonably placid. He sprawled in his chair as before, contemplating his long legs which he'd thrust before him, and smiling softly to himself. And thus the minutes ran on.

Rocky Lynch said at last, "What in thunder is keeping Floren? It shouldn't be taking all this time to talk that saddle-tramp into having a fortune handed to him on a platter. Confound it, the whole business is loco! How could Chance Corday have left his ranch to a man he never saw?"

Floren came in just then, his thin face blank, and he seated himself behind his desk and began hunting through its drawers. Sam Weaver, yawning, said, "Where's the heir unapparent, Otis? Shouldn't he be at this gathering? You said you were going to read Chance's will. The heir should be faintly concerned."

"Malone?" Floren smiled. "By the way, that's his name. Melody Malone. And he's not a saddle-bum, as you've suspected. He's a troubadour. He took pains to explain the difference to me. Also, he offered to sing me a ditty about some girl on Chowder Crick. A man of talent, that Malone."

"What in hell," Rocky Lynch demanded, "is a troubadour?"

"Malone can explain much better than I can," Floren said. "You'll likely be seeing a great deal of him, Lynch. He's over at the hotel right now. I put him up in a room and exacted his promise to stay in town till I have the chance to explain the full circumstances to him. I thought it better not to have him in on this initial reading of Chance's will. I want you gentlemen, and Miss Corday, to fully understand the decision I was entrusted to make before I confer with the man who qualified. But perhaps I sound incoherent. Here, Chance Corday's will can speak for itself."

Dallas Spade said, "By the way, Floren, did Hardin and McTeague ride out of town?"

"They're over at Jake's," the lawyer said, fishing his glasses from a case and perching them upon his long nose. Clearing his throat, he shook the folds out of a legal document, the crackling sound explosive in the silence that suddenly fell. Then he began reading. His voice droned on interminably, droning at last to a finish. Looking up, he smiled. "Well — ?" he said.

"You're still not making sense," Rocky Lynch snorted. "That language is your'n, not Chance Corday's. There's mention of Miss Corday, and mention of Dallas and the crew — and that I can savvy. But I'd like you to put the rest of it in plain language."

"Miss Corday, to the best of Chance's knowledge, was his only living relative," Floren said. "The will explicitly states that there's to be a home for her on the C-C Connected as long as she wishes to remain, and that twenty-five per cent of the ranch's profit is to go to her."

He ticked this point off on a long finger. "Dallas Spade is also provided for. In view of the loyalty he has given the spread, he's to hold his foreman's job as long as he wishes. Also, he's to get a bonus each fall, the amount to be consistent with the showing of the ranch for the year. The same consideration is to be shown the crew to a lesser degree. They may keep their jobs if they desire. Subject to the provisions I've mentioned, the heir is to be in full charge; all matters of policy will be of his choosing."

A bony finger sought out a passage in the will. " 'And the heir shall be designated by the executor of this will who will base his choice upon the following consideration: whoever shall first indicate by word of mouth or appropriate action an open defiance of a person known locally as Quirt Hardin shall thereafter be considered as the heir.' Gentlemen, isn't that plain enough?"

"What he means, Rocky," Sam Weaver said lazily, "is that Chance died without actually naming an heir. The point is that the first person who actually squared off to Quirt Hardin was to get the ranch. And it was up to Floren to judge who the qualified party might be."

Floren said, "When we were gathered here a while ago, Lynch, you suggested that we give Quirt Hardin a fight — to cut his fence if necessary. You'll remember that I said it was very important that I know exactly what you meant. In other words, I had to understand whether you were talking bluff or actually talking war against Hardin. You backed water, and by that narrow margin you missed inheriting the C-C. It should be obvious now why I couldn't discuss the terms of the will. Anybody might have been tempted to try qualifying."

"It's loco!" Lynch shouted. "How in thunder could a man leave his ranch to somebody he's never seen? It would be just as crazy if I wrote a will saying that after my death my ranch was to go to the first red-headed galoot who walked through my gate!"

Floren smiled. "There have been stranger wills than that on record, Lynch. In fact the subject of odd wills would fill a book, and for a number of years I've contemplated writing one. Chance Corday was of sound mind when he made his will. He had an idea in the back of his head, and he was taking the only way he knew to ensure that idea's success."

"Sound mind!" Lynch muttered. "And he leaves his ranch to a stranger!"

"Chance had his eyes open wider than the rest of us," Floren said patiently. "He saw Quirt Hardin come to the Cinnibar and buy up the acreage that became the nucleus of his Curling Quirt. He saw Hardin add to that acreage by whatever means were the handiest, and he watched Hardin's bunkhouse fill with hard cases who were little better than hired thugs. He spoke to me of these things, and I pooh-poohed at his fears. Even when Hardin brought in surveyors, I could see nothing sinister in the move. But Chance Corday did. And it was about that time when Chance came to me and had his will drawn up. Yes, the legal language is mine, but the idea was Chance's."

Dallas Spade said, "Now it's beginning to make some sense. Chance wanted an heir who would have already proved that he wasn't afraid of Quirt. It doesn't make me happy to think that Chance estimated me so low."

"Chance thought a lot of you, son," Floren said kindly. "That's why you're mentioned in the will. But he was afraid the shadow of Quirt Hardin had fallen too broadly across you. You see, while Chance had watched Hardin grow, he'd also watched the rest of us cower at the sight of him. Even a fighting man like Lynch here, only *talks* war. That's the way Hardin's intimidated all of us. It was going to take an outsider to lead a fight against Hardin. There was trouble coming. Chance could smell it a mile off. Maybe he had a hunch he'd get a bullet in the back when things really broke. Instead, he died in an accident; but when he died, the one man with the nerve to really buck Hardin was gone. And Chance had known it would be that way when he passed on. So he played as safe as he could by leaving his ranch to a man who would fight. You might say that Chance Corday bequeathed the war that was coming when he willed away the C-C Connected."

Spade said, "And you figure this saddle-tramp is the man Chance wanted?"

"He's the man who qualified. Chance wasn't called by his name for nothing, and that was the chance he had to take when he drew up his will. You all heard Hardin order Malone to fetch back Breed Lenoir. You all heard Malone refuse.

"That was defying Hardin, and that was what the will specified."

"Something queer there," Sam Weaver said thoughtfully. "Hardin shooting at that big yellow cat."

Floren spread his hand in a gesture of finality. "It was for me to choose. I chose as the will specified. Melody Malone takes over the C-C Connected as soon as I've explained matters to him. You've seen the man, and you know what he's done since he hit town. I want you to keep him in mind. Because whatever you south range ranchers choose to do to buck Quirt Hardin's scheme, you've got to do it together. And that means you've got to consider Malone from here on out."

Weaver came to his feet. "It's been quite a day," he said. "*Quite* a day. Me, I'm getting a bite to eat and riding south. Coming along, Rocky? There's a time for action and a time for meditation. I'm going home and meditate — unless my wife finds some chores for me."

Lynch said, "I'll ride along with you, Sam. I've had enough for one day. Next thing you know, I'll be seeing jack rabbits chasing coyotes. Chance was loco, I tell you. Plumb loco!"

Dallas Spade waited until the echo of the boots of the two had faded in the hallway, and then he said, "A will can be broken, can't it, Floren?"

The lawyer had come out of his chair and was standing by the window, his hands locked beneath the tails of his coat. Turning now with something akin to anger in his eyes, he said, "Don't you think you've done pretty well, Spade? Chance Corday took you in, a drifting cowboy, and gave you a riding job. In due time he raised you to foreman over the heads of older men. When he made his will, he insured your job and lined you up for a bonus. Isn't that enough to wring out of his will?"

Spade coloured. "You don't savvy. I wasn't thinking about busting the will to get myself a bigger slice. I was thinking of Miss Corday. By all that's sensible, the C-C Connected is really hers."

"Then I'd like to have her speak for herself," Floren said with a show of heat.

Anita had spoken not one word during the reading of the will or afterwards, and with Floren's eyes upon her she hesitated. "We'll leave it as it stands," she finally said. "After all, I was a stranger to Uncle Chauncey. That he remembered me at all is more than I expected. He acted according to his judgment. I think it best to back his judgment. I only hope you picked the right man, Mr. Floren."

"The will could be broken," the lawyer admitted. "There is always the question of sound mind, and, in the case of a freak will like this one, it can be argued that the very terms of the will indicated an unsound mind at the time of its preparation. But I know what Chance Corday wanted. I've picked my man, and I'm standing by him."

"That should be good enough for me, I reckon," Spade said. "You've got me wrong, Floren. I backed Chance Corday when he was living, and I'll back his judgment now that he's dead. But what do we really know about this Melody Malone?"

"He went up against Breed Lenoir with an empty gun, and he knocked the stuffings and the spirit out of him."

Spade smiled. "While you were talking to Malone after the ruckus, I spoke to some of the fellows who were crowding the walk over in front of Jake's Eating Place. Malone's going into the Elkshead was one of Jake's poor jokes. Jake sent him over there to get himself a free bite to eat. Malone didn't know what he was up against until he got into the saloon. Any man will fight when his life is at stake."

"But he bucked Hardin afterward."

"I'm still wondering if that proves anything, Floren. To a stranger, Hardin is just a big, fat man with a big, loud mouth. Isn't there an old saying about fools rushing in where angels fear to tread?"

"Malone didn't bat an eye when Hardin reached for his gun," Floren persisted. "And every one of us — including Malone — must have thought that Hardin was going to use that gun on him."

"Malone didn't have much choice as I see it," Spade argued. "Everything happened too fast. Some men jump when a gun starts clearing leather. Some men freeze. How are you going to measure a fellow by a thing like that?"

Anita had been studying Floren's face, and she said now, "You had another reason, Mr. Floren. You haven't mentioned it, but I've a feeling that these arguments you've been making have merely been to sustain your judgment. I'd like to know what really made up your mind about Melody Malone."

"A little thing," Floren admitted. "A very little thing. Yet something about it told me that here was the man Chance Corday had had in mind. His gun, Miss."

"His gun was empty," Spade interjected. "He told us he'd swapped his cartridges to pay for stabling his horse."

"That's just the point," Floren said. "He swapped his cartridges. *But he kept his gun.* Don't you see? He knew that sooner or later he would get more cartridges, so he kept the gun. Which means that he sensed someday he might need that gun. Now whether Malone was aware of it or not, that, I maintain, was the thinking of a fighting man."

Chapter V
"I Want Him Dead!"

Melody Malone, stretched out in unaccustomed luxury upon a bed in the Belle Fourche, Stanton City's most pretentious hostelry, stared at a crack in the ceiling and eased the ache of his battered body, reflecting the while that this was doubtless the craziest town in Montana. Loco — lengthwise and crosswise. First of all, there'd been that air of desertion when he'd ridden in; you'd have thought the place was a ghost town. Then there'd been that restaurant man who'd sent him into the Elkshead as a joke — a joke that had pitted Melody against Breed Lenoir. A fine sense of humour they had hereabouts! And Lenoir had been crazy, too — kill-crazy. What a handful that gent had turned out to be! Melody ached with the memory.

Such had been his introduction to Stanton City, and after the fight, that fat man had come who'd wanted him to call back Breed Lenoir and who'd gotten plenty poisonous because Melody hadn't been of a mind to obey. The fat fellow had even grabbed for a gun — but he'd started shooting at the big yellow tom-cat Melody had toted into town. Crazy! But the lawyer fellow had topped them all.

The lawyer — what was his name? Florid — ? Florian — ? — had followed Melody into the saloon when Melody had gone back after his silver-plated guitar. And the lawyer had plucked at Melody's sleeve and introduced himself and started babbling about Melody being the heir to a large ranch. They'd done considerable talking, but it had only gotten Melody more confused. When this fellow — Flowers? — had fetched him to the hotel and put him up here, he'd made Melody promise to stay until they could talk some more. It had seemed best to humour the man. And when Floren, or whatever he called himself, had left, he'd laid currency on the bureau top and muttered something about Melody maybe needing it to take care of current expenses!

The money was still there; Melody could see it from where he lay, and it was real enough. If it wasn't for that, Melody might have doubted whether all this had actually happened. The bruises Lenoir's fists had given him were real enough, too. And here he was, stretched out upon a bed and apparently a man of importance, for the hotel manager had twice poked his bald head through the doorway to ask whether Mr. Malone required anything to add to his comfort. Melody had determined to shy a boot at the fellow if there was a third appearance, but the manager must have been warned by the gleam in Melody's eye.

So now Melody lay in comparatively blissful contemplation of the queerness of this town and its populace, and he packed no grudge against anyone until his thoughts flitted back to Jake. A joke was a joke, but sending a man up against Breed Lenoir was the sort of thing that helped fill cemeteries. He had a score to settle with Jake, and the thought of the man reminded him that he, Melody, still hadn't eaten. In the ensuing excitement he'd forgotten that it had been hunger that had sent him into the Elkshead. But now he was a man of means.

Swinging his long legs from the bed, he slid into his boots, hoisted his belt and holster from a chair and latched the belt about his middle, adjusted his sombrero, and pocketed Otis Floren's money without counting it. Coming down a carpeted hallway, he descended a carpeted staircase and crossed a lobby strewn with horsehair sofas and chairs. The afternoon was far gone as he stepped to the boardwalk, and when he reached Jake's Eating Place, the supper trade had begun to filter in. Jake was behind the counter, and he gave Melody a wary look as the troubadour parted the screen doors, but Melody only grinned, and Jake decided to match the grin. There was an empty stool at the long counter, and Melody would have settled for that, but Jake instantly called to the lone waitress who was also his wife. "Fix up a table for this here fellow."

Then he turned his toothiness upon Melody once more. "Glad to see you again, stranger. Mighty glad. I used you a mite rough, I reckon. There's a free meal on me."

Melody nodded. "You figure that squares up everything?"

"Samantha!" Jake bellowed. "A new tablecloth for our guest."

Mrs. Jake, a slatternly object who looked like a sack of grain tied in the middle, hastened to obey. Customers were looking up, and Melody was getting even more attention than on the occasion of his first visit here. Ushered to the table, he seated himself, and Samantha stood waiting, brushing a stringy wisp of hair from her forehead. But Jake himself took over.

"You name it; I'll fetch it," he announced expansively.

"Now let's see," Melody mused. "We'll start out with a stack of flapjacks, and I like my syrup on the thin side. Then bring me an order of ham and eggs. That will take care of breakfast. When I've mopped up the eggs, fetch a steak and fried spuds and coffee. We'll top that off with roast beef and mashed spuds and some apple pie. And more coffee."

Jake's pendulous jaw sagged. "Now just because the meal's free —" he began to protest.

"It's supper time, and all I've eaten to-day you could put in your eye," Melody explained patiently. "So I've got three meals to catch up on, and I'm doing it. One's free; the other two I'll pay for."

Jake's grin was restored. "That's fair enough," he agreed. "Mighty fair."

The food began coming, and most of it was to Melody's liking, but the syrup wasn't thin enough. He fixed that by pouring water into it and stirring it with his fork handle, and when the waitress came to clear away the leavings of breakfast before fetching the next meal, Melody clung to the syrup pitcher. "Might like some on my roast beef," he explained, turning a solemn face to her startled look.

He was nearly an hour at eating, and dusk was falling when he tilted the last cup of coffee. Jake approached the table again. "Anything else?" he asked.

"Why, yes," Melody said. "I'd like a funnel."

"*A funnel?*"

"A funnel," Melody patiently repeated. "Haven't you got one around somewhere?"

Shaking his head, Jake vanished into the rear part of his establishment, and meanwhile Melody signalled the waitress, handed her currency, paid for two-thirds of what he'd eaten and got his change. When Jake returned, bearing a tin funnel, Melody was tossing a quarter into the air and catching it. Taking the funnel Jake extended, Melody said, "Watch!" Leaning back in his chair, he thrust the funnel into the waistband of his Levis, tilted back his head and placed the two-bit piece with diligent care upon his forehead. When he brought his head slowly forward, the coin slid, tinkled against the brim of the funnel and fell inside.

"How do you like that for a stunt?" Melody inquired.

Jake had watched sceptically. "It don't seem so hard."

"A dollar says you can't do it once in five tries!"

Gingerly Jake took the funnel and thrust it inside the waistband of his own trousers. "Sit down," Melody urged. "You'll be steadier." Jake placed the coin upon his own tilted forehead, and by then every customer in the place was neglecting his food to watch this odd tableau. And with every eye on Jake, Melody quickly seized the pitcher of watered syrup and emptied it into the funnel.

Jake came erect with a roar, tipping his chair over in his haste, and he was staring down at his splotched trousers when Melody slapped him. An open-palmed blow, it left the marks of Melody's fingers on Jake's swarthy cheek, and then Melody slapped him again, on the other cheek. There was a glint of laughter in Melody's eyes, but little of humour in his tone. "That squares us up," he snapped. "The first slap was for sending me over to the Elkshead to get myself killed. The second was to remind you to go easy if you ever get tempted to play that kind of trick on somebody else!"

Brushing past Jake, who was almost blind with anger, Melody headed for the door. Jake started after him, but the syrup was seeping down his legs, and he had to walk all aspraddle. Lifting a hairy fist, Jake shook it, his voice trembling with rage. "This ain't the finish between us!" Jake bellowed. "I'll even up if it's the last thing I ever do!"

But his only answer was the slamming of the screen doors as Melody went out through them. The restaurant had turned uproarious with laughter, and the sound was music in

Melody Malone's ears as he went walking back toward the hotel. . . .

It took a big horse to carry Quirt Hardin, and as he rode southward to his ranch late that day, he used his spurs with more than ordinary savagery. McTeague, riding silently at Hardin's side, was hard put to keep abreast of the man. They had tarried in Stanton City a couple of hours after the incident of Breed Lenoir's departure; they had had a bite at Jake's place and looked into the various saloons and listened to the talk of the town; and very little of what Hardin had heard had been to his liking. All in all, the day had been a sour one with everything going wrong, and so Quirt Hardin's horse suffered. For Hardin was a man trying to ride away from his own thoughts.

Out of Stanton a wagon road wound across the tawny, autumn-browned range; the smell of sage was in the air, prairie chickens stirred in the brush, and off in any direction could be seen the dark blotches that were grazing cattle. It was a road to be ridden slowly and with a deep appreciation, but neither man had an eye for its pastoral beauty. Quirt Hardin had been too busy all of his life to have developed a taste for anything that didn't have a dollar sign affixed to it; to him grass meant money, no more, no less. McTeague's blindness was of another sort. A man who lived dangerously; his was an alert consciousness that saw every coulee as a place of ambuscade, every brush clump as a menace. And so they came through the lush serenity of the dying day, sullen and silent and immune to all else but their own thoughts.

In three directions the Cinnibar Hills lifted pine-crowned heads, brown and dark blue blending into purple, their sprawling immensity transformed by the coming of night. Those hills seemed to draw no nearer as the miles fell behind the two riders, and at last the pair topped a rise to look down upon the Curling Quirt buildings. Here Hardin showed his first spark of interest in his surroundings, sitting his saddle for just a moment while his lathered horse caught its wind. Those buildings below were sprawling and pretentious — a low, gallery-fronted ranch-house, a long bunkhouse, a bright red barn, a scattering of corrals, a blacksmith shop — and they were the proof of Quirt Hardin's prosperity and therefore good to his eye. Light glowed in the bunkhouse; in the yard stood a wagon heaped high with coils of barbed wire. With a grunt Hardin prodded his jaded horse into action again and came down a gentle slant to a stop before his ranch-yard gate.

"Take supper with me, McTeague," Hardin said. "I want to talk to you afterwards."

McTeague acknowledged the invitation with a nod and turned his reins over to a man who materialised out of the shadows. Most of the crew were in the bunkhouse, and, from the sounds, a lively poker game was in progress. The horses led away, the two entered the ranch-house, coming into a room strewn with Navajo rugs and littered with costly furniture that didn't match. Hardin, sprawling in a chair, raised his voice to a bellow that fetched a peg-legged pirate who was the Quirt's cook. When a meal was finally spread upon a table, Hardin ate in the sullen silence that had held him since leaving Stanton City; and afterwards he beckoned McTeague to follow him and led the way to a pair of chairs upon the gallery.

The night was perfection. A canopy of stars winked high above them, the Cinnibars were vague and solemn and wrapped in the dignity of darkness. Close by a horse stamped in a corral and nickered softly; far away a coyote sang its mournful lullaby, distance softening the weirdness of that lament and turning it into something remote and lonely that made the building more comfortable. Then Hardin spoke, and the night was spoiled.

He said, "You heard the talk that went

around town after Lynch and Weaver came out of Floren's office the second time, Mac. Granting that everybody who passed it along added ten per cent to it, there still must have been some truth behind it. Do you suppose Corday really left his ranch to the first hairpin to buck me?"

McTeague busied his lean fingers at fashioning a cigarette. He sat deep in his chair, a dark-garbed man almost lost in the shadows, but Hardin could see that McTeague's gun had been hoisted around so that it remained close at hand. The scrape of McTeague's match broke the silence; for a moment his inscrutable face was a bleak etching in the flare. "Likely," said McTeague and drew upon his cigarette.

"So Floren handed that stranger the C-C just because the fellow refused to call back Lenoir when I asked him to," Hardin mused, but petulance was in his voice. "And now we've lost Lenoir. Did you ever see such a beaten dog as Breed was when he rode out?"

"Breed'll ride back," McTeague said.

"Maybe. Lenoir won't take that licking and like it. He'll hate that stranger as he's never hated anybody before. The question is which will be the strongest — his fear or his hate."

"With Breed it'll be hate."

"I wonder," Hardin said. "It doesn't much matter. There isn't a ten-year-old kid in Stanton who wouldn't spit in Breed's eye after today. Mac, the cards all turned up wrong for me today. But the worst thing I did was to let that cat spook me."

"That was bad," McTeague agreed.

"But it was so confounded unexpected, seeing that big yellow monster show up from under the porch. It didn't give me time for thinking. I just acted."

"You had more than one shell in your gun," McTeague observed pointedly.

"I see what you mean," Hardin decided after a moment of silence. "I should have shot the stranger. But you notice he didn't try for his own gun. That would have made me a murderer in Anse Crain's eyes. The sheriff would have jugged me for sure. No, Mac, the time hasn't yet come when we can forget to be careful. A few more months, maybe, and I'll hold the sheriff and the rest of this range in my hand. But the sign wasn't right to go shooting a man who wouldn't draw."

McTeague sent the cigarette arcing away; it made a swiftly moving red eye in the darkness and showered sparks when it landed on the ground before the gallery.

Hardin said, "Chance Corday was our big stumbling block, Mac. Chance was as human as the next one, and his skin wasn't any more bullet-proof than yours or mine. But Chance stood for something on this range. That's what made him a real menace. He stood for leadership — for the kind of guts Sam Weaver has never had and Rocky Lynch only thinks he's got. With Chance to lead those south ranchers, we might have run into big trouble fencing off The Strip and charging toll. You see what I mean?"

"Corday's dead, boss."

"Sure he's dead. But even in dying he saw there might be a chance to beat us. Look at that crazy will of his. Some deep thinking went into that, Mac. Do you get Chance's idea? A man who bucked me was a man who proved it could be done. That's going to give Weaver and the rest of them something to think about. Which is exactly what Chance knew it would do. That stranger's become a symbol. And it's up to us to change that symbol."

"Meaning, boss — ?"

"Meaning that we've got to get him. We haven't any choice. Maybe the stranger didn't know who I was when he bucked me. Likely when he learns the kind of figure I cut on this range, he'll be sorry he brushed my fur the wrong way. But he won't back water; he's a saddle-bum who's won a ranch by defying me, and he'll figure he's got to keep on defying me to hold that ranch. That's neither here nor there. It's the example he sets that's bad."

"You want him dead?"

"I want him dead!" Hardin snapped. "But there's more to it than merely bushwhacking him some dark night. He's got to die in such a way that everybody will know the Curling Quirt tacked his hide on the wall for him. Yet that way has got to be such that Sheriff Crain won't be riding out here with a warrant. Now that's going to take some figuring. We may have to wait for our opportunity — but we can't afford to wait too long. Just keep turning this little matter over in your mind, Mac. There's got to be a way."

"I'll find the way," said McTeague.

Chapter VI
Boss of the C-C

Being a celebrity began to pall on Melody Malone after the first few days. By virtue of his fight with Breed Lenoir, his defiance of Quirt Hardin, his acquisition of the C-C Connected, and his revenge upon Jake, his fame had spread like wildfire. And rumour elaborated all the tales that were told about him. In the Elkshead of a lush evening, the talk had it that Chance Corday's will contained a clause whereby Melody Malone was to marry Chance's starchy-looking niece who was also putting up at the Belle Fourche. It was likewise told that Chance's will had definitely named Melody Malone, and that the guitar-toting stranger was, variously, a Cattleman's Association detective, and ex-Texas ranger of horrendous fame, a personal representative of the governor sent in to check up on Quirt Hardin, and a famous reformed outlaw who'd built a reputation under another name.

Thus, whenever Melody ventured upon the street, he was critically surveyed by women, carefully measured by men, and awesomely haunted by troops of small boys who dodged his heels. His ridding the town of Breed Lenoir had made him friends, but, since everyone persisted in looking upon him as a freak, he had no means of basking in the warmth of this friendship. And he had one enemy in the town. Jake. The restaurant proprietor proved to have a one-way sense of humour, and Jake refused to forget that funnel incident. When Melody appeared at the restaurant for breakfast the next morning, Jake had greeted him with a brandished meat cleaver, and Melody had discreetly taken his patronage to a Chinaman down the street.

Mostly, though, he kept to his hotel room. Otis Floren had called on him that first evening and carefully explained about Chance Corday's will and gone into a rapt description of the present worth and future potentialities of the C-C Connected. Also, the lawyer had explained about The Strip and Quirt Hardin's scheme which threatened to throttle the south ranchers. Anita Corday had been present at that meeting, but she'd said practically nothing. Melody had listened with polite patience to Floren but showed no unbounded enthusiasm over the gift destiny had presented him.

Since then Melody had spent a great deal of time stretched upon his bed or curled in a chair with his guitar cuddled against him. As the days ran on, he managed to conceive a good many new verses about the gal on Chowder Crick, and thus he had the pride of achievement. Also, he learned that if you stare at that crack in the ceiling from a certain angle, it looked like the profile of an exceedingly ugly man.

From time to time he'd seen Anita in the hotel hallway, and they'd done no more than exchange nods. Her room was down the hall from his, he discovered, and she spent most of her days behind a closed door. Accordingly, his surprise was genuine when he answered a knock on his own door one morning and found her standing there. He'd been expecting the hotel manager, and he had one of his boots ready in his hand. Anita had swapped her tailored suit for a divided riding skirt, a shirt and jacket and a high-crowned sombrero, and she'd let her brown hair down so it fell upon her shoulders. The changes made quite an improvement.

"Dallas Spade sent one of the C-C hands in this morning," she said. "The fellow fetched word that the ranch-house is just about in shape for me to move in. I'm hiring a buggy to carry my baggage out to the ranch. I wondered if you'd like to come along?"

Melody was hopping about the room on one foot and trying to pull his boot on to the other foot, but he managed to say, "I'd like that fine."

They came out of the hotel together and proceeded to the livery stable where Melody selected a light buggy and a team of matched blacks, and he also paid the additional fee that had accrued against his own saddler and hitched the mount behind the buggy. Brutus, the big yellow tom-cat, was in the stable, perched upon a bale of hay and purring himself silly. Melody scratched the tom under the chin and said, "Take care of yourself, old-timer."

When he tooled the buggy back to the Belle Fourche and picked up Anita's suitcases and stowed them behind the buggy's seat, the girl said, "You're moving to the C-C, too, you know. Aren't you taking your own things along?"

A jerk of his thumb indicated the guitar slung across his back. "All packed," he grinned.

The guitar placed alongside Anita's luggage, he climbed to the seat and took the reins, and when they'd rolled along the main street and across the railroad tracks near the shipping pens, the girl directed him to the proper road.

The morning was like wine; the range lay brown and endless and smelling of autumn, and there was a slight haze in the air, and beauty was everywhere. They rode in silence the first few miles, Melody busy with the reins and Anita sitting with her chin cupped in her hands, drinking in the countryside. At last she said, "Mr. Floren tells me he's tried several times to get you to go out and look at the C-C. He says you've never seemed interested."

"Reckoned the ranch wouldn't run away," Melody said. "What difference if I got there on a certain day or a week later?"

She said, "You're an odd fellow. If it weren't contrary to human nature, I'd suspect that inheriting a ranch doesn't mean a thing to you."

Melody shrugged. "No need to get in a lather about it."

A frown darkened Anita's face. "But think! You're getting something that most men have to work a lifetime for, and you're having it handed to you through a freak of luck. Is that so bad? Or would you rather keep drifting around, just being a . . . a saddle tramp?"

"A troubadour, Miss," Melody corrected her.

"Have you always been a troubadour?"

"Worked as a cowhand when I was younger," Melody said as soberly as though he were fifty years old instead of half that age. "Then

I took to roaming around with my guitar. Didn't know I was a troubadour at first. A bald-complected professor told me I belonged to an ancient and honourable profession. It got started in what he called the Gothic Age. The troubadours were kings and nobles and knights who made up poems, put 'em to music, and sang 'em to win fair ladies. It was them that gave the world the idea that woman is a finer, nobler creature than man. And that wasn't all. In an age when most people were either plundered to death or taxed right down to their shoelaces, music was the one thing that was free and belonged to everybody, and the troubadour was the man who fetched it to the people. There's worse work in the world."

He pressed the reins into her hands and reached behind the seat for his guitar. A chord plucked from the instrument, he began to sing:

"Yup, I know a gal on Chowder Crick,
Homely as a hedge-fence, duller than a stick,
Hi, yo, diddle, di, day. . . .
But her pappy's rigged with a gold mine claim,
And me I could use a little of the same,
So I'm gettin' fixed to marry up with that dame,
Hi, yo, diddle, di, da-a-a-y. . . ."

Anita laughed gaily. "Your own composition?"

Melody nodded as he put the guitar behind the seat again and took the reins. "Words and music," he admitted. "Reckon it won't ring down through the ages, but when I sing it folks grin and start tappin' their toe on the floor. You figure these big cattle ranchers do more than that for folks?"

Anita said, "You're not going to trick me into any argument about the relative values of materialistic and spiritual things. But what does it get *you*, mister? Town talk has it that you landed in Stanton City with a lone dollar in your pocket."

Again Melody shrugged. "It's a big world, and I reckon I haven't covered much of it yet. But there's always one more hill to climb, one more town to see. That's what fetched me to Stanton. Lately I've been wondering what's wrong with my head, letting myself get sidetracked this way."

Anita said, "I notice your cartridge belt is studded with bullets. It was empty the first time I saw you."

Melody grinned. "Mr. Floren advanced me some money. Seemed like I should spend part of it so I wouldn't hurt his feelings. The clerk in the mercantile store figured I was getting myself prepared for the attentions of a fellow named Jake. This Jake's been threatening to shoot me when the sign is right."

Anita, who'd lifted her eyes along the road, suddenly pointed. "Look!" she cried.

They were approaching The Strip, but Melody, none too well acquainted with the country, hadn't realised that. Otis Floren had gone into a lengthy description of the Cinnibar for him, but it was the sight of Quirt Hardin that made Melody realise his present whereabouts. Off to the east, a quarter of a mile from the wagon road, fence posts had been set, and barbed wire was being strung by means of the wagon wheel method. Spools of wire had been mounted on axles in a wagon bed, and as the wagon was driven along the fence line, the wire unreeled. When a distance of about two hundred feet had been covered, the wagon was stopped and its wheels braced. With one hind wheel jacked up, the strung wire was fastened around its hub. A Curling Quirt cowhand turned the wheel, thus stretching the wire taut. Another hand was busy stapling the tightened strands to the fence posts. Sitting his saddle and supervising this process was Quirt Hardin himself, and at his stirrup was his ever present shadow, McTeague.

Hardin, seeing the wagon wending out of the north, spurred toward the road, and Melody sawed on the reins. Hardin smiled an expansive smile and doffed his sombrero. "Good morning, Miss Corday," he said. "And . . . er . . . Mr. Malone. That's the name, isn't it? I've heard a great deal of talk about you in Stanton City."

"Don't let it lather you," Melody said. "It's probably a pack of lies."

"Otis Floren's word is unquestionable, and he admits that you're the heir to the C-C Connected." Hardin's smile grew even wider. "I understand that I was, in a sense, the instrument of your destiny. You should remember me kindly for that, Mr. Malone."

McTeague had reined up at Hardin's elbow, but the gunman sat his saddle, saying nothing. Anita said, "Have you stopped us to collect toll, Mr. Hardin?"

Hardin made a gesture with the fat hand from which his quirt dangled. "The road is open to travellers. I'm no highwayman, you know, and not nearly the ogre that Otis Floren has probably painted me. I've got the south border of The Strip all fenced, but there's a gate where the road cuts through. Likely you'll find one of my men posted there, but I assure you that you'll not be stopped." His eyes turned back to Melody. "You're moving out to the ranch to stay, Mr. Malone?"

Melody shrugged. "One place is as good as another for roosting."

"You must call at the Quirt sometime. Both of you. I'm a man who believes in being neighbourly. Good day to you."

He went wheeling back to the fence-builders, McTeague following after him, and the buggy rolled onward. Anita said at last, "An odd man, Hardin. There's a warmth to his personality at times that makes him the pleasantest man I've ever known. Yet I heard him speak of his scheme to collect toll for crossing The Strip, and I know he'll back up his play. Steel beneath velvet, that's him."

Melody hunched his shoulders. "B-r-r," he said. "Did you ever look into the eyes of that McTeague? Pale milky white they are, and they never left me all the time I was talking to his boss. I'll swear McTeague aims to eat me the first chance he gets — eat me up and wash me down with coffee."

When they reached the far side of The Strip, they found the gate Quirt Hardin had mentioned, and they found a hardcase Quirt rider squatting near it, a rifle across his lap and his sombrero down over his nose. But this sentry wordlessly came to life and opened the gate and let them through, curtly acknowledging Melody's nod as he did so.

Now they were into the southern half of the Cinnibar, and Anita, who'd been here before, pointed off into the distance. "Yonder are the holdings of Rocky Lynch and Sam Weaver. The road forks toward their places somewhere along here, but we keep following the main road. We should be sighting the C-C Connected before long."

And they came upon the buildings within the hour. This was like a hundred ranches Melody had seen — a low ranch-house, a barn, corrals, outhouses, a long bunkhouse. There was an air of neatness about the place, and a clump of cottonwoods to shade it. When Melody wheeled the buggy before the ranchhouse, Dallas Spade came down the steps from the gallery to greet them and to lend his hand to assisting Anita from the buggy. Spade wore a working cowhand's garb to-day and therefore looked less pretentious than he had in Otis Floren's office, but it was plain that he'd carefully shaved this morning, and it was also plain that Anita's coming was a pleasure to him.

"We haven't rebuilt all of the inside of the ranch-house," he said, "but I've got a bedroom fixed up for you, Miss Corday, and I reckon you'll find things fairly comfortable, though there's still a smoke smell inside. Malone, you won't mind sleeping with the rest of us in the bunkhouse for the time being?"

Melody nodded. "You mentioned a smoke smell. Did the place have a fire?"

Anita replied. "You'll remember that Mr. Floren said Uncle Chauncey had died accidentally. A fire gutted the inside of the ranchhouse, and he was killed in it. He's buried up yonder on the bluff."

"A fire? How did it start?"

"We don't know," Spade said. "We'd just started our fall round-up, and the crew was out on the range. Chance was here alone, in the house. Just by luck, I came back to the ranch that night on some business or other, and I saw the flames. The inside of the place was an inferno. I tried to get to Chance, but the flames drove me back. I just about killed a horse getting out to the crew, and when I fetched them here, we rigged up a bucket brigade and saved some of the house. We've been rebuilding since."

Spade paused, obviously embarrassed and not liking the thing he now found necessary to approach. "We called off the fall round-up to get the house back into shape for Miss Corday. Now I've sent the boys out on to the range again. I took it for granted that that would be O.K. all around."

Melody said, "You don't like me, do you, mister?"

Spade coloured, then recovered himself. "No, I don't," he said bluntly. "I've got nothing against you personally, but I reckon you're sitting in the spot Miss Corday should be holding down. I'm not quarreling with Chance's will, but I've still got to be convinced that Otis Floren made a smart choice. And that's why I'm asking you right here and now what you propose doing as boss of the C-C?"

"Doing?" Melody smiled vaguely. "Why, I reckon I'll let you have the handling of the ranch. Corday wanted you kept as foreman which proves you must be mighty capable."

"But when the cattle are rounded up — ?" Spade said, and it was obvious he was asking about The Strip and the trouble that might accrue when it was necessary to cross that land.

"We'll worry about that later," Melody said. "I never saw any sense in borrowing trouble ahead of time. Say, do any of the hands here play musical instruments?"

"Musical instruments!" Spade looked as though he were about to strangle. "How the hell do I know? I never asked them when we hired them. Come to think of it, Shorty Jenkins totes a mouth organ around with him."

"A good start," said Melody. "I was thinking that when the round-up is over and we sort of get holed up for the winter, maybe I could organise a cowboy band among the crew. Yes, sir, our own little C-C orchestra. Now how do you like that for an idea, Spade?"

Chapter VII
Death in the Afternoon

Round-up time on the Cinnibar. A cook's alarm clock noisily announcing the dawn on a milk pan turned upside down. Cowhands rolling out of tarps. Another day. Riders combing the draws and the coulees; riders hazing cattle to the bedding grounds; riders sweating and cursing and risking their necks for forty a month and found. The white tilts of a chuck-wagon against the sky-line. The brown drabness of the gather held upon a flat. Gimlet-eyed reps from other ranches searching a herd for their own brand. Dust . . . chaos . . . clamour. . . . A white moth of a moon smiling upon nightherders singing to the bedded beasts. The chuck-wagon fire burning dimly and winking out to darkness. A horse nickering in the remuda. A coyote yapping its discontent to the moon. The teeth of winter in the air. Fall round-up. . . .

Across the Cinnibar, from high brown hills

to high brown hills, there was activity. The C-C Connected was the farthest behind in its work, for C-C hands had toiled at crude carpentry within the gutted ranch-house to the detriment of other things. Now, with Anita Corday installed in the ranch-house, the crew was out on round-up, and from the higher land they could see the gather of Sam Weaver's Anvil and Rocky Lynch's Lazy-L. Those neighbouring riders had amassed a considerable amount of beef, but the C-C was rapidly equalling the Anvil's gather. Sam Weaver, from a cowboy's viewpoint, was a good man to work for. There was much in Weaver's philosophy that would have fitted him to be a Mexican; indolent and easy-going, he saw no reason to do to-day what could just as well be done to-morrow.

Not so Rocky Lynch. Year after year he was invariably the one to reach the shipping pens first; he took a certain pride in winning a race with neighbours who were not even aware that there was a race. That was Rocky Lynch's way. Big, blocky, and explosive, he always worked clumsily but with a gusto that got results. This year he was pushing his crew with more than customary vigour and rapidly earning their anger by a sullen attitude on his own part that manifested itself in many ways. Rocky Lynch was a man with a secret regret and a gnawing worry, and these were putting their mark on him.

His foreman, one Horseface Hennessey, bowed of leg and aged in the saddle, stopped Lynch at the chuck-wagon one morning and said, "Damned if I can quite see this all-fired rush, boss. We'll have those cattle gathered in jig time, but Hardin's already got the south side of The Strip fenced off, and a man posted at the gate. Why hurry our gather when we can't move them to town anyway?"

Now this was touching the very core of Lynch's worry, and it brought the colour to his red-veined face. Ever since that day in Stanton City when Melody Malone had ridden in, Rocky Lynch had been reflecting on the dark ways of destiny and reminding himself that the right word at the right time, the proper show of a courage he would have to command sooner or later anyway, would have made him the master of the C-C. Aye, that was a bitter pill to swallow! He might have qualified as Chance Corday's heir, and he hadn't. So now his anger rose readily, and he said, "I'll get through that fence!"

"But how, boss?" Hennessey queried patiently. "You're going to be ready to move to the shipping pens away ahead of Weaver and the C-C bunch. If you figger on having us rush that fence with wire-cutters in one hand and six-shooters in the other, we'll want all three crews behind us. Hardin will give us a fight. And he can ask Sheriff Anse Crain to back him in that fight. The law will be on the side of the Curling Quirt."

"To blazes with Weaver!" Lynch snapped. "I've told you what he said in Otis Floren's office. Weaver wants to talk soft to Hardin and try to get him to lower his toll, and the only ace Weaver will have to play will be to bluff that we'll take our cows south through the Pass of the Blackrobes. Hardin won't bluff. He knows that our going through the hills would run so much tallow off our stuff that we'd be money ahead to pay the toll."

Hennessey shook his head. "I still figger Floren had the right idea. Whatever we do, the three spreads should do it together. What about this Malone jigger? They're still talking in Stanton City about what he did to Breed Lenoir. You reckon he might have an idea or two about how to bust up Hardin's game?"

Lynch grew apoplectic. "Him! I rode over to their gather yesterday. Figgered I'd have a talk with Malone. And what do you suppose he asked me? Did I play a musical instrument? *A musical instrument!* Wants to organise a band if he can find enough talent hereabouts. That's all he's got in his fool head. Music! *Faugh!*"

Hennessey had pitted himself against the

stubbornness of Rocky Lynch in the past, and the foreman could recall no time when he'd been able to put a dent in his boss's inclinations. So Hennessey shrugged now and said, "Mind lettin' me in on whatever you've got in your head?"

Lynch cast quick glances to left and right. "We'll play our hand alone," he said guardedly. "And that's just where we'll fool Quirt Hardin. He'll be expecting we'll all string together, so he won't figger there can be anything in the wind until the last ranch has finished its gather. But one of these nights soon, we'll be moving our cows north. We'll go through that fence like Sherman went through Georgia. Let Hardin do his hollering to the law afterwards, if he likes. I'll take my chances on a lawsuit. And meantime my cows will be rolling east to market."

Again Hennessey shook his head, but he held his tongue. He reckoned he was getting old, Hennessey did. Maybe it was time to retire. But that took money. Now what in thunder had he done with last summer's pay?

In Jake's Eating Place in Stanton City, a man could always count on finding two things — flies and Jake. For Jake took his meals in his own restaurant, lived in quarters behind the place, and there were those who argued that if Jake ever got beyond the confines of his own establishment and into the fresh air, he would instantly collapse and it would then be necessary to fry a steak and waft its greasy odour into his nostrils to restore him. Even the town's medico subscribed to this weird belief.

Therefore it was with some surprise that Jake's wife, Samantha, that same slatternly woman was also the restaurant's waitress, found him preparing one afternoon to foray beyond the screen doors. And Samantha was not one who was usually disturbed by anything Jake did. Years of association with him had inured her to this odd sense of humour and to the greasy look of him and filled her with a stolid contempt for this mate of her choice. She had come to Jake ten years before in search of a job and had been given one, and a romance of expediency had flowered in the kitchen. A justice of the peace had done the job and taken his fee in the form of a meal ticket. The only change that had been made in Samantha's life was that although she continued to be Jake's waitress, there was no longer any salary connected with it.

To-day she watched silently as Jake donned clothes that were usually kept carefully tucked away in a closet. Jake had once seen a picture of a famous Parisian *restaurateur* who specialised in a soup which had enraptured crown heads, and Jake, who usually squeezed a dollar until it screamed for help, had gone hog wild in a lust to be garbed like this professional brother. The outfit consisted of a pair of striped trousers, a dark coat cut long in the tail, a white waistcoat, a flowing tie, and a derby which a horse could have stepped on without doing any damage. While he climbed into this outlandish layout, he hummed a little tune, which raised Samantha's eyebrows. Jake had been mighty hard to live with since the day he'd discarded a pair of trousers into which a pitcher of syrup had been poured. He'd even taken to muttering dire threats in his sleep, and the mere mention of Melody Malone's name was enough to renew his anger. But now he was happier than a sparrow in a livery stable's lot.

"Where are you going?" Samantha finally demanded.

"For a little ride," Jake said vaguely, examining himself in a cracked mirror. "Out to the Curling Quirt, say."

"Hardin doesn't owe you any money."

Jake hoisted his dark brows. "Of course not, my sweet. But who knows? Perhaps he might be willing to share his wealth with me."

"You're crazy!" Samantha decided.

"You remember Hardin shooting at that

tom-cat the other day, my sweet? Did you ever wonder why the sight of Brutus spooked our fat friend?"

"A lot of folks have been wondering. I suppose *you* know the answer."

Jake chose to look very mysterious. "There isn't much that fools me," he said. "I'll try to get back before the supper rush. Take care of things, my dear."

Fifteen minutes later found Jake heading out of Stanton City aboard a rented livery stable saddler, an incongruous figure as he perched upon the horse. Following the same wagon road Hardin and McTeague had taken from town he jounced across the tawny rangeland, one hand clutching his derby, the other holding the reins wrapped around the saddlehorn, while the miles became an agony to him. He was sure his spine was going to be driven up through the top of his head, for a good deal of daylight intermittently showed between him and the saddle. But he comforted himself with the thought of what might result from this journey, and when he topped the last rise and looked down upon the Quirt buildings, he regarded their opulence with almost a possessive interest.

Hardin lolled upon his gallery, keeping to its shade and enjoying the afternoon with a fat man's indolence that was backed by a feeling that things were going extremely well. A Quirt hand who carried field glasses had just ridden to the ranch, made a report of all activities to the south, and departed in the direction of the C-C Connected. The strip was nearly fenced, and there was no hurry about Quirt's round-up, for it was the one ranch that could move its cattle to town whenever it pleased. Seeing Jake coming down the slant, Hardin turned to McTeague who sat silently beside him, and said, "Now what in thunder do you make of this?"

McTeague gave no answer; he was carefully appraising Jake, and even Jake's weird get-up failed to bring a smile to the gunman's face. Jake reined to a stop before the ranch-yard gate, acknowledged Hardin's invitation to light and sit by grinning expansively, then climbed to the gallery and found a chair. Lowering himself into it, he groaned.

"Not used to riding," he explained.

"What fetches you this far from town?" Hardin asked.

Jake had had a good many miles for rehearsing the speech he would make when this question was put to him, but now, sitting beside Hardin and with the presence of McTeague like a dark shadow on the day, the courage fled from Jake. Clutching at it by putting his mind to easy dollars and the diverse ways in which they might be spent, he said boldly, "Brutus, Quirt."

"Brutus — !"

"That big yellow tom-cat."

Hardin's eyes narrowed until they were nearly lost in folds of flesh. "Just what in thunder are you driving at, mister?"

"Well, now," said Jake, "you've maybe heard tell that that big tom is just crazy about fish. Sometimes we have them on the bill o' fare, but usually we don't, because I ain't much of a hand at wasting my time beside a creek when beef is so easily got. But the whole town sort of takes an interest in Brutus's welfare, and we'd like to see him get a feed of fish once in a while. So I've decided to raise a fund by popular subscription — said fund to provide Brutus with fish; I've put you down for five hundred dollars. Fair enough?"

All the good humour had gone out of Quirt Hardin, and his voice turned flat and harsh. "That will buy an awful lot of fish, mister!"

Jake shrugged. "It all depends upon how you feel about Brutus."

Hardin said, "Just exactly how much do you think you know, Jake?"

Again Jake shrugged, and in his heart at this moment was a great fear and a wish that he'd never conceived such an idea. But boldness had served him well so far, and he decided that a continued display of it was his only weapon. "Enough, Hardin," he said. "I know enough. Do you think I'd have come out here on a bluff?"

"That's *just* what I'm thinking," Hardin said.

Jake came to a stand. "Well, now, if you don't want to subscribe to the fund, I'll be getting along. Maybe Sheriff Anse Crain will put up some money. He always sort of liked Brutus. But I was thinking that if you had five hundred dollars handy, Quirt, I wouldn't have to bother anybody else."

Hardin arose too, and for a moment Jake was certain the man was going for his gun. But Hardin raised a fat hand to his fat throat, and he caressed himself as though he were easing the bite of a hangrope, and in Hardin's eyes was more fear than any other man had ever seen there. He dug his hands into his pocket and produced a wad of bills, and from this he untangled five one hundreds. Extending these to Jake, he said, "There, damn you! Now get off the place and don't ever show back here. I've played your game once but don't think you can bleed me. There won't be a second time!"

Jake took himself away with considerable alacrity. Stuffing the five hundred into his pocket as he went through the gate, he mounted the rented saddler and made it up the slant with his heels beating hard at the cayuse's flanks. The two on the gallery watched him go, Hardin still caressing his throat. "Was he bluffing, Mac?" the Quirt owner demanded. "That's the question! Was he bluffing?"

"Mostly," said McTeague.

"But we can't be sure. And we can't have him running around loose if he's guessed the truth. His tongue swivels at both ends. He couldn't keep a secret if he was paid every day."

"I'm going after him," said McTeague.

"You reckon that's best?"

"I'm in on this," said McTeague, in a manner that settled the matter, and he left the gallery, disappearing around the house in the direction of the corrals. Five minutes later he streaked past the house and headed up the slant in the direction Jake had taken, but once having topped the rise and sighted Jake far out across the dun drabness, McTeague changed his course, dipping into a coulee and racing his horse the length of it. He knew this range, did McTeague, and he showed a canny skill at keeping to cover, while, at the same time, he manoeuvred to place himself ahead of Jake. This took considerable doing, and it was an hour later that he sat his saddle in the shadow of a low butte, waiting patiently beside a trail that would sooner or later bring Jake to him.

And it was thus that Jake found McTeague. After that first frantic flight from the Curling Quirt, Jake had, of necessity, let his mount come from a gallop to a walk, and with the widening of the distance between himself and Hardin's headquarters, some of Jake's courage had been restored. After all, he'd fashioned a scheme that had worked, for wasn't he departing with the money? Naturally Hardin had given it to him with a threat and a display of temper. That was to be expected. But five hundred dollars was five hundred dollars. Maybe, Jake reflected, he should have asked for a thousand. The chances were he would have gotten it as easily. But there could be another time, in spite of Hardin's threat. After the fall round-up, say, when Hardin was well fixed with ready cash. Or when Hardin had collected toll from his neighbours to the south and would be in a mood to consider that easy come, easy go, wasn't such a bad swap.

It was a good day, and a good world, Jake decided. He began humming his little song again, and he considered enlarging his restaurant and fell to estimating the extra profit that might accrue from a dozen additional tables. Samantha would have to hump herself a little faster in the enlarged establishment, but it wouldn't hurt the old girl. Maybe he'd buy her a present out of this windfall that had come to him to-day. A new comb, for instance. He'd noticed that the one she used had several missing teeth.

And then his dreams went winging, and the song died in his throat, for he had rounded the butte and he found McTeague blocking his path. McTeague said nothing, and no words were necessary. What McTeague intended was written in his milky eyes, and if that wasn't plain enough, there was a levelled six-shooter in his hand. That much Jake saw, and then the six-shooter spoke, and the bullet, catching Jake in the chest, blew him from his horse. He was dead when he hit the ground.

The livery-stable horse, gun-shy, bolted, and McTeague, without a glance at Jake, went after the mount. Catching the horse, he fetched it back to where Jake lay sprawled, and the black-garbed gunman dismounted then, turned Jake over with his toe and went through Jake's pockets. The five hundred dollars removed, McTeague studied the fallen man for a long moment and then began hoisting Jake's body to the back of the livery-stable horse.

That took considerable doing. The horse had got the smell of death in its nostrils and it shied violently, and at first McTeague considered blindfolding the mount, but he managed without having to do so. His own lariat lashed Jake in place, and McTeague turned back towards the Curling Quirt, taking the same route he'd followed, keeping to the cover of coulees and draws.

It was nearly dusk when he reached the buildings, but before he approached the ranch-house, he tied Jake's horse off at a distance. Hardin was awaiting him on the gallery, and Hardin said, "You get him?" McTeague merely nodded. He jerked his thumb to where he'd left the horse. "Yonder," he said.

"Yonder?" Hardin cast an anxious glance about him. "You don't mean you fetched his carcass back *here?* Why didn't you dump him into a coulee and roll some rocks on him? He's bound to be missed in town, and Anse Crain will come hunting."

"So I figgered," McTeague said and made what was a long speech for him. "You want to get Melody Malone. You said we'd have to get him the safe way. Looks to me like opportunity is knocking right now. Walk off a piece with me, and I'll tell you what I mean."

Chapter VIII
Thunder to the South

A thought, planted with a man, can be forgotten and still have its insidious way of growing. So it was with Melody Malone in his first days as boss of the C-C Connected. The thought had been given roots by Dallas Spade when the foreman had bluntly declared that he considered Melody to be usurping a position rightfully belonging to Anita Corday. Melody had done no smarting under the implication, but the notion that he was not wanted and was far from popular on the ranch lingered in the recesses of his mind, giving its own dark colouring to all that happened thereafter.

Until his coming to the ranch, Melody had taken the matter of his inheritance as a dream which might as well be enjoyed since there seemed to be no awakening from it. A madman named Chance Corday had left a queer will whereby an utter stranger had fallen heir to

Corday's vast acreage. A madman named Otis Floren had selected Melody as the heir and put money in his pockets. An entire town had turned equally crazy in accepting these strange circumstances. So Melody had drifted with the winds of destiny. Drifting was his habit; he was a tumbleweed by nature, and if he'd become snarled in a golden fence with diamond-studded posts, there was no reason to complain.

He'd been stepping on nobody's toes, Melody argued. Otis Floren had told him that anybody objecting to the will would find it a simple matter to break it. Anita Corday, according to Floren, was perfectly satisfied to abide by her dead uncle's queer way of doing business, and Anita had shown no animosity toward Melody. Everything was as snug as a bug in a bearskin rug.

Until Dallas Spade had spoken his piece.

Melody, installed in the bunkhouse with the crew while Anita moved into the partially-restored ranch-house, had met the C-C crew and found them an assorted and salty lot. They had all shaken hands solemnly and then proceeded to leave him to his own devices. Under other circumstances, he might have presumed this to be natural enough since he was a stranger among them and occupied a position above theirs. But he sensed an animosity, whether it existed or not, and that was because of the planted thought.

When the crew rode out on round-up, Melody went along, but, in spite of the fact that he'd ridden for a few brands in his day and knew the ways of a working cowboy, he didn't make much of a hand for the C-C. If a cow had to be hazed from some brushy coulee, there was always a man there ahead of Melody. If a songster was needed to quiet the bedded gather of a dark night, Spade, in his capacity of foreman, always selected an amateur. Melody seemed to have become nonexistent.

These things, too, might have appeared to him in a different light. The C-C hands were a close-knit crew, used to working together, and familiar with the ways of each other. They exemplified an efficiency of which Melody might have become a part in time, but in these first days he was, naturally, the extra spoke in the wheel, the third thumb, the man who didn't fit in. Friendly and gregarious by nature, Melody might have worked at making himself one of the outfit, and likely he would have succeeded. As it was, he drew apart, feeling alien and unwanted and suspecting that he was on a par with the polecat in the estimation of the C-C men.

Then Dallas Spade sought him out one evening when the crew was gathered around the chuck-wagon. "I wish you'd head back to the ranch-house, Malone," Spade said. "At least at nights. Somebody should be there, and I reckon you're it."

Melody said, "Do I crowd you fellows?"

Spade frowned. "There's room on this Cinnibar range for all of us to sleep without rolling on each other, but I don't like the idea of Miss Corday being alone at the ranch. There's no reason for Quirt Hardin to strike at us; his game will be to sit tight behind his barbed wire and wait for our move. But, just the same, I'd feel better if there was a man around the spread."

Here, again, was something that might have appeared normal to a man with an unshadowed mind, but once more Melody had the feeling of being an outsider. He could have refused Spade's request; he was still boss of the C-C Connected, and Spade was only the foreman. But instead, Melody caught up his own horse, turned his back upon the bedded gather, the chuck-wagon, and the round-up crew, and headed for the empty bunkhouse. Light glowed cheerily in the nearby ranch-house when Melody reached his destination, but he didn't make his presence known. Putting up his horse, he took his choice of the bunks and went to sleep.

He saw Anita the next day and offered some

vague explanation for his being at the ranch. He'd decided not to trouble her with Spade's fears. But the girl had a bit of news of her own. She said, "You know, I'm convinced that this ranch is being watched. Yesterday I was sure I saw sunlight reflecting from field glasses from a bluff to the north. Do you suppose Quirt Hardin is having an eye kept on all of us so he'll know when the south range ranchers are ready to start moving cattle to town?"

That was likely, Melody agreed, but he refused to be concerned about Quirt Hardin. People hereabouts had made quite a character out of this Hardin fellow, but, as Melody saw it, Hardin's sinister stature was mostly in their own fears. In his few days with the C-C round-up crew, Melody had met both Rocky Lynch and Sam Weaver who had ridden over at one time and another. Behind Lynch's blustery manner and Weaver's casual acceptance of the fall of the cards, he had read the same vague, unworded fear, and he'd seen it in Dallas Spade's mien, too. Otis Floren had spoken at length about Hardin, but Melody had been unimpressed. There was murder in Hardin all right; Melody had seen it in the fat man's eyes when he'd defied Hardin before the Elkshead Saloon, but looks had never killed anyone. In Melody's mind, a bear was a bear only when he bit you. He had yet to feel Quirt Hardin's teeth.

And so he sat around the bunkhouse feeling quite useless, but he did manage to wrangle a little music out of his guitar, and he made up more verses about the girl from Chowder Crick, but they seemed to lack the old sparkle. And then, quite suddenly, he remembered the thing Dallas Spade had said that first day he, Melody, had come to this ranch, and he thought then that he understood everything — the crew's aloofness, his own inability to work with them, and his present banishment back to the ranch.

He wasn't wanted here. In the crew's eyes, for doubtless they felt as Spade felt, he was an interloper, a man who took advantage of a dead man's distraught last wish in order to steal the bread and butter out of a pretty girl's mouth. And so thinking, all the fun went out of being the heir to the C-C, and the golden fence with the diamond-studded posts became just an ordinary fence, blocking him from further drifting and making him miserable. And then he saw the simple way by which all this could be changed.

Turning up the bunkhouse lamp, for the darkness of his second evening here was gathering, he found paper and pencil and began to work on a letter. When it was finished, it read:

Dear Mr. Floren:

I reckon there's nothing in the law that says a man has to keep an inheritance just because he gets it.

I've been in this one place so long now that I'm beginning to look like a Cinnibar gopher. I'm hankering to find one more hill to climb, one more town to see. So I'm leaving.

The ranch goes to Miss Corday. If it's really mine, like you said, I take it for granted I've got the right to give it away. Dallas Spade will make her a good foreman and do the man's work around here. He's a good fellow and handy with cows. If just *giving* the ranch to her isn't legal enough, you can draw up one of those papers that says, "for one dollar and other valuable considerations I hereby transfer title." Or whatever it is those papers usually say. This note will give you the power to act for me and do the right thing.

I owe you for the money you gave me, and I'll send it to you first chance I get.

Yours,

Melody Malone.

He left the letter lying on the bunkhouse table. Dallas Spade would find it there and see that it got to Floren; Melody had no doubts about that. Silently saddling up at the corral, he adjusted the guitar on his back, slid his holstered forty-five around so that it wouldn't bite at his leg as he rode, climbed into the saddle and walked his horse until he was well past the ranch-house. Then he headed due north. He looked back only once, just before a turn of the trail dropped the ranch-house from his sight. Once again the light glowed cheerily, and he smiled, and smiling, sighed. This was his good-bye.

Alone with his thoughts, he kept his cayuse at a steady, mile-eating pace that soon brought him over a hump of land and near the fence that marked the southern border of Quirt Hardin's Strip. There'd be men patrolling the wire these nights, he supposed. If it were true that Hardin had been spying on his neighbours, then Hardin would know that any time now the other ranches would be ready to move cattle, and Hardin, accordingly, would be prepared. None of which concerned Melody. He was a lone traveller, bent upon business which in no way menaced Hardin, and therefore he didn't expect even to be challenged at the gate. And even when horsemen loomed out of the night before he reached the gate, Melody had no more than a normal curiosity about them.

There were a half-dozen riders in all, and, big among them, was Quirt Hardin himself, with McTeague at his side. The starlight was bright enough for Melody to recognise them both, and the others, he supposed, were Curling Quirt hands. But one horse had what appeared to be a dead man draped over its saddle, and it was this sight that gave Melody his first alarm. Rearing back and tugging at the reins, he brought his saddler to a halt, but he was almost upon the group as he did so, and instantly they were surrounding him. He felt the pressure of a gun-barrel grinding against his ribs, and somebody quickly lifted his own forty-five from its holster.

Anger sharpened Melody's voice. "What in blazes is the big idea?"

McTeague had taken Melody's gun, and McTeague now fired the gun, aiming it at the sky and triggering only once. Some of the more skittish horses reared, but the Curling Quirt hand who had the drop on Melody was able to keep his gun against Melody's side. Hardin reined close to the troubadour and smiled. "Here's rare luck," Hardin said, but he spoke to McTeague. "No long trip to the C-C Connected. The mountain has come to Mahomet. Tie his hands, boys!"

There was no use in struggling; Melody

could see that. His gun was gone, and the odds were heavy, and to try fighting or running would only net him a bullet. He let his hands be lashed behind him, and then Hardin said, "Remember that big cottonwood over yonder?" and waved a fat hand to the west.

They went riding then, somebody snatching at the reins of Melody's horse and leading it along, and they moved silently, that burdened saddler with its grim load trailing them; but Melody could get no real look at the dead man. Nor could he guess what lay in store for himself. The mention of a cottonwood had not as yet suggested the truth to him, and his questions got him no answers. Quirt Hardin was deep in thought, and, with the fat man leading the way, the group came to where a giant cottonwood kept a lone vigil, its gnarled branches tracing a weird pattern against the night sky.

They halted in the shadow of this cottonwood, and yonder Melody could see Hardin's fence marching from east to west. They were just south of The Strip. Hardin raised a fat hand for attention, and said, "Our running into Malone changes the picture, boys. This is going to be a lot better than just dumping Jake's carcass near the C-C ranch-house. Mac, I reckon you know what I've got in my mind. You had the same scheme when you fired Malone's gun. Hang on to that gun."

McTeague nodded, and Hardin said, "Here's the story, boys, and listen careful because every one of you will have to tell the same yarn to Sheriff Crain later. We were riding along, patrolling our wire and keeping as quiet as we could just in case somebody was sneaking around with a pair of wire-cutters. We heard voices, and we heard Jake and Malone, here, sitting their saddles and making fighting talk. Stanton City's been laughing about the grudge Jake bears this Malone gent, and Jake was all heated up. One word leading to another, Malone uncorked his gun and shot Jake out of his saddle. That's where we took a hand. When we looked Jake over, the poor devil wasn't even packing a gun. That got us mighty peeved. We all knew Jake pretty well, and Malone's a stranger, an outsider. In fact we got so peeved we just hauled Malone to the handiest cottonwood and hung him. Now when the job's done, we'll take Jake into town and tell that story. Have you all got it straight?"

Men nodded, and Melody sat rigid in his saddle, knowing now what was in store for him and seeing the tightness of Hardin's careful scheming. Those field glasses Anita had seen flashing! Hardin had known that Melody Malone was the only man at C-C headquarters, and Hardin had intended leaving Jake's body on Melody's doorstep. But that hadn't proved necessary. Once again Quirt Hardin was seizing opportunity and twisting it to his own use. No use in telling the fat man that he, Melody, was no longer boss of the C-C. Hardin had already gone too far, and Hardin would hang him anyway.

And this was the moment when Melody Malone saw Hardin as the others on Cinnibar Range saw him, and at last he knew Hardin for what the man was. But the knowledge was coming too late for any earthly use, for McTeague had uncoiled a lariat and was sending the rope swishing over a low-hanging limb of the cottonwood. The noose, falling earthward, was seized and placed about Melody's neck. Melody began fighting then, but there wasn't much he could do, not with his hands tied behind him. A jerk on the noose almost strangled him, took the fight out of him, and McTeague, dismounting, kept the rope taut as he lashed its other end around the bole of the tree.

"Slap his horse, somebody," McTeague said.

He gave this order with all the casualness of a man to whom this sort of thing was an everyday chore to be performed in a routine way. But the man who suddenly held Melody's attention was Quirt Hardin, for even in the faint starlight it seemed that Hardin's face had taken on a stricken look. One of Hardin's hands strayed to his throat in the same gesture he'd made when Jake had threatened him with some secret knowledge that very afternoon, and even though Melody hadn't been present then, he recognised the fear that, strangely, was in Hardin now. Hardin said sharply, "That won't be necessary, Mac. We'll all ride off a piece and wait. In a short while his horse will start grazing and move away from him."

McTeague shrugged. "O.K.," he said.

And here was the unbelievable, and even with the imminence of death uppermost in Melody's mind, he was impressed by this queer quirk in Hardin's nature. The fat man had an unholy fear of hanging — a fear so strong that Hardin could callously commit another man to the hang-tree but couldn't bear to witness his victim's death. It was on a par, Melody supposed, with some men's inability to stand the sight of blood. But, surprising as it was, it held no shadow of hope, for Melody was to hang anyway, whether Hardin watched or not.

The group was turning away, leaving Melody to the inevitable that would follow when his horse moved out from under him. And at that moment McTeague suddenly raised his hand, commanding silence. *"Cattle!"* he said and quickly dismounted again, coming down to his knees and pressing his ear to the ground. "South!" he announced. "A big herd."

Hardin stiffened to attention. "Just as we thought," he barked. "One of them's figuring to move through the wire by night. Rocky Lynch, I reckon. His gather was the nearest finished." His eyes singled out one of his men. "You, Charley, take Jake's body and head to the sheriff with it. Tell him that story just as I told it a few minutes ago. And tell Crain I'd have come to town, but that just after we finished hanging Malone, we had to ride to protect our wire. Tell him he'd better get out here and give us a hand. The Strip's legally ours, and we've got a right to the law's protection. Mac, give Charley Malone's gun to turn over to the sheriff for evidence."

He glanced at the others. "Come on, boys."

They all went roaring away, all but Charley who led the horse bearing Jake's body along the fence toward the gate. Soon the last man had been swallowed by the night, and Melody was alone, sitting his saddle with his hands bound behind him and a noose taut around his neck.

Already his horse was restless. The mount had stirred slightly when Hardin's crew had lifted their cayuses to a gallop, and only the quick pressure of Melody's knees had kept his own horse standing. But how long could he control the animal? He fell to talking to the cayuse, using soft, cajoling words, begging it not to stray, but the horse lowered its head and began cropping and moved a step forward, the noose tightening around Melody's neck. Horse sense, Melody decided bitterly, was an overrated commodity.

The sweat was standing out on him now. Hardin had taken no chances by riding away and leaving him here still alive. Hardin had known that it would be only a matter of time, minutes perhaps, before Melody would be doing a death dance upon air, and Hardin had gambled that there wasn't one chance in a thousand that anybody would come past this lonely spot in the meantime and save Melody. No, Hardin had delt himself nothing but aces, and a few more minutes would finish the game.

That thunder to the south was growing louder. Cattle running in the night. Now Melody could hear a distinct shouting, the thin popping of guns. Blast Rocky Lynch for a hotheaded fool! Had the man thought to tackle the fence alone when he might have had three crews at his back instead of one? It sounded like there might be a fight going on yonder, and Melody wondered if the Quirt hands had stampeded Lynch's cattle, turning them back upon the Lazy-L crew. But no, that thunder was going louder, which meant the herd was moving toward the fence. Lynch, then, had likely stampeded his own herd, meaning to sweep them through the fence by brute force even though the vanguard of the herd would be piled up on the wire and cut to pieces.

For a moment Melody's spirits soared. Were they coming this way? Would some Lazy-L hand spy him here and recognise his predicament? Then the hope turned sour. The Lazy-L hands would be *behind* that herd. And if the cattle were heading this way, as the growing thunder indicated, then Melody's own horse would be caught up in the stampede and swept along. And he'd be left dangling from the limb of this cottonwood — dangling a few feet above the ground in the path of the stampede!

Chapter IX
Blood on the Barbed Wire

Whatever fetched Dallas Spade from the round-up camp to the C-C Connected ranchhouse that night, it was not the reason he gave the crew. To them he mumbled something about wanting to see the boss on a matter of business, and, having made this excuse, he threw gear on his own saddler, lined out past the bedded herd, and kept at an easy jog toward the distant headquarters of the ranch. Actually, he had no desire to see Melody Malone, and no business to transact with the C-C owner. To Spade, Melody was a hopelessly impractical man and of little consequence. Any policy concerning the disposal of the herd once the round-up was finished would be formulated by Spade himself. This he knew. Malone had advanced no plan nor showed the slightest interest in the problem that confronted the ranch; and placed the responsibility squarely upon Spade.

The truth was that Spade wished to see Anita Corday, though the foreman had covered half the distance to the ranch-house before he realised what had made him so restive this evening. Anita had gotten into his blood. When she had first come to Stanton City a few weeks back, fetched by a letter from Otis Floren, Spade had been impressed by her. Another man might have admitted that this was love at first sight, but Spade had never been in love, and he wasn't sure that he was now. A man of ambition and of foresight, he had given women no place in his scheme of things. Women, he had observed, were either the means of a man squandering his pay, or else they were an anchor that kept him fastened to monotony. Someday, Spade had supposed, he would marry. But there were other dreams to be realised first, and none of them were romantic.

The world, as Dallas Spade saw it, was peopled by two kinds of men — those who took orders and those who gave them. As a working cowhand, he had soon decided which type he wished to be. His star fixed for him, he had taken to drifting, looking always for the shape of opportunity, and he had found it on the C-C Connected. Chance Corday had liked him, and Corday had raised him to foreman, and thus Spade had taken his first big step. Now it was he who gave the orders. He, in turn, still took them from Corday, but there might be a day when that would be different. Spade had learned patience.

Destiny had intervened with a whirlwind series of events — a burning ranch-house, a funeral on the C-C, a reluctance on the part of Otis Floren to discuss Chance Corday's will. And then Anita had come. Anita, according to Stanton City's guess, was Chance Corday's heir, and Anita was a lovely woman if you took a second look at her. Spade had considered the circumstances, and taken that second look. If a man were to get married someday, he might do worse than marry Anita Corday. The man who married her would be the boss of the C-C Connected.

But Chance Corday's freakish will had changed all that. By Corday's wish, a stranger, a saddle-bum whom Corday had never seen, had become the master of the C-C acreage. The cash value of Anita Corday had thereby been decreased; but still Spade hadn't been able to shake her from his mind. And that was why, to-night, he was riding toward the ranch. He was going to court, though he didn't know exactly how a man went about it. He had mastered much learning in the span of his years, but there was this blind spot in his education.

When he looked upon the C-C buildings, he saw that the bunkhouse was dark but that light glowed in the ranch-house. That meant Malone was spending the evening with Anita, and Spade named himself a fool for having sent Melody in from the round-up camp when he might have kept the man out there. But that decision of Spade's had been prompted by a genuine concern for Anita's safety, and also by a desire to rid himself of the sight of Malone. And now he was to have the man underfoot all evening.

Dismounting before the bunkhouse, Spade turned his horse, still saddled, into a corral, then ran his hand experimentally over his lean, handsome face. A shave would be in the line of an improvement, he decided, and he went into the bunkhouse, lighted the lamp, and cast a look around for his razor. That was when he spied Melody's note. Picking it up he read it, then re-read it, and when he'd finished it a second time, he'd forgotten about shaving.

He went quickly to the ranch-house and thumped on the door, and when Anita opened it and stood framed in the doorway, he cut off her ejaculation of surprise at sight of him by silently extending the note. She, too, read it twice, and then stood staring at it, saying nothing.

"I had him pegged wrong," Spade said. "I

figured he intended taking advantage of the will by hanging on to the ranch but that he aimed on letting the rest of us do the work and the worrying. But now he's ridden away from the whole deal."

Anita said, "I saw him around earlier this evening. He can't have gotten very far away. If we hurry, we can fetch him back."

For a moment Spade stood as though stunned, trying to understand the perverseness of female reasoning but finding nothing in it that made sense. "But he won't want to come back," he finally managed to say. "Don't you savvy? He sees this the same way the rest of us saw it. He knows that the ranch should really belong to you, and he's done the one thing that will right matters. The man had a bigness to him that I was too blind to see."

But Anita was brushing past him and heading toward the corral, and Spade had no choice but to follow her. Her intention was all too plain, so Spade snaked out a horse for her and got gear on to it, and while he was working at this, she said, "You think I'm crazy, of course. Perhaps I am. I can see what Malone is trying to do, but I won't have it! His giving the ranch to me doesn't change the fact that Uncle Chauncey left it to *him*. Do you remember what I once said in Mr. Floren's office?

All of you wanted to know what I'd do in regard to the ranch, and I told you I wanted to act as my uncle would have acted. If Chauncey Corday had wanted me to have this ranch, he'd have left it to me. But Uncle Chauncey wanted it in the hands of a certain kind of man. Melody Malone qualified. He *can't* just ride away from all this!"

Spade said, "Maybe Malone figures the ranch isn't worth the fight. Maybe that's why he's running out."

"That isn't the way his note reads," Anita said as she stepped up into her saddle. "Come on, if you want to help me catch him."

A man who's been surprised so many times in the last few minutes that he'd grown numb from the shock, Spade dazedly mounted his own horse. He had seen a note wherein a penniless man had casually given away a valuable ranch. He had heard a girl refuse the gift on the grounds that a relative now dead had wished matters otherwise. Obviously both the man and the girl were crazy. And with this first glimpse of something that approximated a kinship of spirit between Melody Malone and Anita Corday, Spade wondered how great was the girl's real interest in the man. Was there another more intimate reason why Anita didn't want Melody Malone to ride out of her life? Twenty minutes before Spade would have considered this thought ridiculous. Now he wasn't sure.

And here he was committed to the task of bringing Malone back to the heritage the man had so carelessly thrown away, and he and Anita rode northward, stirrup to stirrup, following the road on the presumption that Melody could hardly have gone any other direction but this one. They rode silently, their hard pace making talking prohibitive, and they held to this high gallop until they were almost to the southern edge of Quirt Hardin's Strip. Here Spade reined down, signalling Anita to do likewise. "Hardin will probably have a guard at the gate," he said. "No use coming hell for leather and letting the Quirt know that something is up."

"If there's a guard, he'll be able to tell us whether Malone passed this way," Anita said.

But they never reached the gate. Not that night. For not long after their brief exchange of words, they topped a rise to look down upon a sweep of land with Hardin's fence running across it, the barbed wire glinting faintly in the starlight. *"Riders!"* Spade whispered, reining to an abrupt stop. "See them down there? Half a dozen of them, or more. And there's only one man as big as that fellow in the lead. Now what's Quirt Hardin doing with the full force of his crew on this side of his fence?"

Anita was peering intently, and it was the faint gleam of starlight on the silver plating of the guitar on Melody's back that identified the man who was Hardin's prisoner and gave her an inkling of the truth. "Melody!" she cried. "They've got Malone down there with them!"

She would have spurred her horse, but Spade got a quick hold on the bridle. "Easy!" he whispered. "They haven't seen us or heard us. Not yet. Let's see what they're up to before we go stampeding down there. The odds are pretty heavy."

Here was wisdom to which Anita had to surrender, and they kept this higher ground then, walking their mounts westward and paralleling the group below. Spade said, "Wish there was a moon to-night. It looks to me like one of those horses is being led. And if I'm not wrong, somebody's been slung over the saddle."

Anita tried looking, but her eyes were no better than Spade's. That something mighty sinister was going on, she now realised, and with that realisation she sensed, for the first time, that she and Dallas Spade might be in danger by virtue of having stumbled upon Hardin and his crew. Obviously Melody was a prisoner, for she could imagine no other circumstances which would be keeping him in

Hardin's company on this mysterious ride. Then she spied the cottonwood below and saw the group pause beneath its gnarled branches, but they became lost in the shadow, and she couldn't see what was going on.

Spade stepped down from his saddle and led his horse below the brow of this ridge before dropping the reins to anchor the mount.

Anita aped the foreman without conscious thought and joined Spade as he hunkered on his heels to keep from skylining himself. She shivered and drew closer to the man, and said, "What do you suppose they are doing?"

"Hanging Malone," Spade said. "Why else would they have fetched him to the tree?"

She'd have started down the slope then if Spade hadn't gotten an arm around her waist, and for a minute the two of them struggled, Anita striving frantically to break free of his grip and Spade hanging on relentlessly. "Stop it, you little fool!" he hissed in her ear. "Do you think I'm getting any pleasure out of having to stand by and watch him swing? But Hardin won't want any guests at this party. If we start down the slope, we'll be dead before we've covered half the distance to the tree. How's that going to help Malone?"

Again she saw his wisdom, and she knew that he was right — dead right. They were doomed to stay here, impotent as an empty gun, watching what went on and powerless to prevent it. Below, those men were talking, but their voices were only a distant babble, a low swell of sound without meaning. Anita lived a thousand agonised years in these minutes, and then she saw the group move out from under the tree, and there was one less of them. "Is he — ? Is he — ?" she said, and thought she was going to faint.

Spade peered hard. "His horse is still under him, near as I can make out. Looks like they're going to leave him that way and let him dangle when his horse starts grazing. Steady, girl! Maybe we'll get our chance to save him after all!"

But Anita had instinctively pulled her eyes away from the gallows tree, for at this moment she heard what McTeague was hearing — that distant, sullen thunder. Spade heard it too. "Cattle!" he cried. "Somebody's moving a herd this way!"

Down below there was sudden, unexpected movement, all of Hardin's men roaring away toward the south-east except one who began paralleling the fence toward the gate, leading that horse behind him whose burden seemed to be a man draped over a saddle. Spade had come erect now; he ran quickly back to where he'd left his horse, and he hit the saddle without touching the stirrups. Anita was slower at mounting, but she managed to be at Spade's side as he whirled his horse about and headed over the crest of the ridge.

"Easy on this slant!" he cried. "Here's a good place to break our necks!"

But Anita was in no mood for caution now; they came down the slope with gravel sliding beneath them, and the horses in constant danger of somersaulting, but even above the clamour of this descent, they could hear a greater noise — the pounding of hundreds of cattle heading up from the south and running now. Off in the distance they could make out dim and mighty movement, but Anita usually had her eye on the tree ahead. They came to the cottonwood at an angle, and Melody didn't see them until they were almost into the shadow of the branches. Spade spilled off his horse and fumbled for a jack-knife. Then he swung up behind Melody's saddle, an action that made Melody's horse rear and threaten to bolt. But Anita was on the ground now, and she grabbed at the bridle of Melody's horse just as Spade cut the hang-rope.

Melody said, "I'm almighty glad to see you folks!"

Spade was sawing at the rope binding Melody's wrists. As he got it cut, he slid to the ground and mounted his own horse. "Let's get out of here!" Spade shouted. "From the sound of things, those cattle are heading this way! Rocky Lynch, I'll bet! The fool's trying to get through the fence."

All three were now aware that guns were banging over yonder to the east, an indication that Hardin's crew and Lynch's were fighting. Spade glanced at Anita and said, "Better head back to the ranch. Sounds like Lynch needs a hand. Why did the idiot try this alone? Now there's nothing left to do but buy into his fight."

And Spade went galloping off to the east, but Anita, instead of obeying his order, galloped after him. Melody was picking up his reins, and she judged that he doubtless would be trailing along, but the things she had to say to him would have to wait. And, so thinking, Anita tried hard to overtake Spade. Ground flowed beneath her; ahead was darkness and clamour and intermittent gunflashes, but when she overtook Spade it was to find that the fight was finished.

Rocky Lynch's plan had been simple. He'd swept his herd at Hardin's fence, stampeding them and planning to send the cattle through by sheer force. And it had worked. Ahead, the fence was a tangled disorder, the posts sheared off, the wire down, and there were dead cattle piled up, testifying to cost of this attempt. The herd had gone on through and was doubtless half-way across The Strip by now; but Hardin's crew sat their saddles in a tight little knot just this side the ravaged fence, and the Lazy-L crew were gathered on the southern side of the broken wire. A strange silence held both groups, a silence made more acute by the diminishing thunder of the vanished cattle.

"What's happened?" Anita asked as she drew abreast of Spade. The foreman merely pointed.

Lynch and his crew had been behind the cattle. And Lynch had reached the fence that had defied him — reached it and gone no farther. He lay sprawled upon the broken wire, his body shapeless as a sack, and his blood glinting on the barbed wire; and this was how his dream had ended.

Spade jerked hard upon his reins, and he shouted across the distance: "See what your damn' fence has done, Hardin!"

Hardin said, "They asked for it. They were trespassing. One of my men has gone to fetch the law. We'll let Anse Crain decide the rights and wrongs here. Unless some of Lynch's boys want to take up where he left off."

But the fight was all gone out of the Lazy-L crew, blasted from them by the bullet that had blasted the life out of Rocky Lynch. Anger edging his voice, Spade said, "Maybe you can make this stick, Hardin, but you're riding to a fall. Not many minutes ago, you tried to hang Melody Malone. We cut him down in time. *He* wasn't trespassing beyond your confounded fence!"

"Malone murdered Jake to-night, Spade. We saw him do it, and we put a rope around his neck. If you freed him, then you cut him loose to put him in jail. Because that's where he'll go when Anse Crain gets here."

"Malone murdered Jake!" Spade twisted in his saddle. "Where are you, Malone? Tell this man he's a blasted liar!"

Anita, too, was looking behind. But there was no movement out there in the darkness. She had supposed that Melody had followed her and Spade on this ride to the scene of battle. But Melody Malone had disappeared.

Chapter X
The Law Looks Twice

Anse Crain had been sheriff of Cinnibar County so long that the smaller fry of Stanton City, too young to have remembered Crain's predecessor, firmly believed that Crain had come into this mortal coil with a sheriff's star pinned upon him, just as Sully Meek, the man who ran the mercantile store, was reputed to have been born with a wart upon his nose. Even the older citizenry had come to accept Anse Crain as a fixture as permanent as the town pump. Come election time, they voted him back into office from sheer force of habit.

All of which indicated that Anse Crain was admirably fitted for his job — and he was. A considerable chunk of man, stoop-shouldered and prematurely bald, he went about his tasks with a stolid, unimaginative efficiency that kept Stanton City a reasonably respectable town. You got no miracles from Sheriff Anse Crain, and very little dramatics, but you got a brand of law that was impartial and thorough. And so, year in and year out, Anse Crain held down the swivel chair in the sheriff's office to the front of the County Jail, a good politician by virtue of the fact that he played no politics; and all concerned were satisfied — with the possible exception of the occasional recalcitrants whom he stuffed into the cells of the huge frame and log building with the barred windows.

Of late though, a careful observer might have detected signs of worry in Crain's rugged face, and, if this same observer had given due consideration to this phenomenon, he would have realised that Crain's worry dated back to the coming of Quirt Hardin to the Cinnibar. Crain, watching Quirt Hardin grow, had played the part of a spectator only; for Hardin had never stepped beyond the law, and therefore Crain's attitude had had to remain impersonal. But Quirt Hardin had the makings of a lot of trouble in him, and this Crain had realised from the first.

Yet Crain could only watch. There'd been Breed Lenoir, of course, and Breed's unsocial habit of terrorising the town, but Crain had been forced to overlook that. On such occasions, since the county didn't expect a lawman to commit suicide for his pay, Crain fetched Hardin from the Curling Quirt to quell Lenoir.

Hardin had always footed the bill for the damage Lenoir wrought — given his hireling a talking to and assured, Crain that there'd be no next time. Whereupon history proceeded to repeat itself.

None of which added up to a major crisis. Boys would be boys, and if you didn't have a nuisance like Lenoir, you had a mighty dull town. Nor could Crain do anything about the other hard cases in Hardin's crew. He had diligently, searched through his file of reward dodgers, hoping to find the face of McTeague among them, but his search had been in vain. It was Hardin's scheme that was slowly greying what little hair Anse Crain still cherished. Crain knew about the scheme, of course, just as all Stanton City had sensed the truth once Hardin had established temporary title to The Strip and proceeded to string fence. And Crain knew that there was much potential dynamite waiting for the fire to be touched to the fuse. It was things like this that were apt to keep a lawman from growing old gracefully.

Yet there was nothing for Crain to do but bide his time. Down south, three ranches were completing their round-ups, and in that same vicinity Quirt Hardin had finished stringing barbed wire. These things Anse Crain made it a point to know. One of these days now there'd be a blow-up. And Anse Crain would have to act in accordance with the laws of the land. That was the trouble with wearing a badge; you had to be so neutral it left you numb. But if ever there'd been a time in his long tenure of office when there'd been blood on the moon, this was surely it.

Therefore Anse Crain worried, and on the night when the fire touched the fuse, he was sitting in his office and reflecting that the raising of chickens would be a mighty comforting business, especially now that the country was getting settled up, and he was estimating how much capital it would take for the original investment. He liked this little office of his. There was only a desk and a couple of chairs and a file and a safe to furnish it, but he could put his feet where he pleased, and he didn't have to mind his language. His home was over on Stanton's Depot Street, and his wife was waiting for him right now, but he chose to linger here.

Lamplight etching the craggy lines of his face, he leaned back in his chair, his boots propped atop his desk; and some men might have thought him asleep. But he was thinking, his mind alternately shuttling from his worry to his dreams, and the one gave a new lustre to the other. He was this way when a man rode up to the hitch-rail before the jail building in late evening, leading a saddler behind him, and when this man framed himself in the office doorway, Crain recognised him as Charley, one of Quirt Hardin's hands. Charley jerked a thumb over his shoulder and said, "I've got Jake out there. He's dead."

That fetched Crain's boots to the floor with a thud. "Jake dead? How?"

Whereupon Charley told his story with parrot-like precision, and Quirt Hardin would have been proud of his man if he'd been there. With a sparsity of words that made the account more graphic, Charley related how the Quirt crew had been patrolling its wire and how they had heard the voices of Jake and Melody Malone raised in argument and had Injuned forward in time to see Jake shot from his saddle. He told this story on the move, for Crain was brushing past the man and going outside to have a look at Jake. His examination made, Crain said, "Who's fetching in Malone?"

"The undertaker, I reckon," said Charley and passed over Melody's gun. "Take a look at this. One shot fired. When we looked Jake over, we found he wasn't even packing a gun. That made us so plumb outraged that we hauled Malone over to that big cottonwood that stands a little west of the road, just south of The Strip, and we strung him up."

"You lynched him?"

Charley began fashioning a cigarette. "Now

that would be for a jury to say," he reflected. "Don't you reckon you'd maybe have pulled on the rope if you'd been there, Sheriff?"

There was this Anse Crain had learnt from many years as a frontier sheriff: only half the laws were written down in the books in Otis Floren's office; the rest were made up on the spur of the moment. If Charley were telling it straight — and doubtless the entire Quirt crew would back his story — then Hardin's bunch had merely done the natural thing at the natural time. Hardin had reason to hate Melody Malone, of course, and a man with half an eye could see the personal touch in to-night's doings; but once again Hardin had played safe. Charley knew it too. There wouldn't be much a jury could do but half-heartedly point out that in the future it might be best for Quirt Hardin to let the county hangman do his own work. Therefore Anse Crain said dismally, "Why didn't Quirt come in himself?"

"The boss has got his hands full," Charley said. "He wants you to ride out to The Strip pronto. Better bring a posse along. Just as we finished putting the rope around Malone's neck, we heard cattle moving north. Rocky Lynch, we figured. The boss sent me on to town, but before I got far, I could hear shooting. Lynch was rushing our fence, and that means we got the right to the law's protection."

There was a bit of irony in this bald-faced admission that the Quirt, having just finished taking the law into its own hands by hanging Malone, now wanted the law of badge and book to stand beside them in a fight against a trespasser; but Anse Crain wasted no time on this reflection. Rocky Lynch was rushing the fence. It had come then, this thing that Crain had expected and dreaded. His own horse was at the hitch-rail, and he lifted himself heavily to the saddle. "Git Jake down to the undertaker's," he told Charley. "And I'm leaving it to you to break the news to his wife. Don't reckon she'll carry on much. Me, I'm heading south before there's more dead men strewed around."

He had ignored Charley's suggestion that a posse be organised. The law's job to-night would be to act as referee; the war was already started, and all the guns on the Cinnibar couldn't stop it now. He left town at a high lope, crossing over the railroad tracks and taking the road south, and he punished his horse on that ride. He measured the miles to The Strip, estimating the time it would take to cover the distance, and he thought of the futility of making this ride at all. Whatever was happening would doubtless be over and done with long before he reached the scene of action. And, so thinking, he topped a rise to look down upon the sprawling, pretentious buildings of the Curling Quirt and knew that his guess had been right. Bunkhouse and ranch-house glowed with light; horses milled in the corrals, and men made dim movement in the yard. The bulk of the Quirt crew was here at the home ranch which meant that whatever had happened at the fence was finished.

Roaring down the slant, Crain swung from his saddle before the ranch-house and spied the bulk of Hardin out near the corral, the ever-present McTeague nearby. Striding toward the two, Crain said, "Looks like some of your crew is missing, Hardin. Don't tell me that Lazy-L guns rid this range of them."

Hardin smiled, lazily flicking the quirt dangling from his wrist. "Just in case somebody else should get the same idea Rocky Lynch got to-night, the rest of my boys are patrolling wire that was wrecked by the Lazy-L. We won't be able to put up new wire until to-morrow."

"Spill it," Crain snapped. "Just exactly what happened?"

Hardin shrugged. "Lynch's scheme was to stampede his cattle through my fence. It might have worked except that all of us were in saddles and watching for something of the sort. There was a fight. I defended my property, naturally. Rocky Lynch stopped a bullet, and that took the heart out of his men. That's all there is to it. Ride over to the Lazy-L, if you like. Horseface Hennessey will tell you the same story. So will Dallas Spade. He and that Corday girl rode up at the finish."

"So Rocky's dead," Crain said and suddenly felt very old.

"Will you be writing up a warrant, Sheriff?"

Crain eyed him in cold fury. "You know I can't do a thing. The law's on your side, and Lynch was taking his chances when he rushed your fence. But I'm not so sure I can't jail you for hanging Melody Malone. Your man told me all about that, too."

"You couldn't make it stick," Hardin said. "You see, Malone is still alive. Dallas Spade came along and cut him down before the rope could get him. And now Malone's hit for the far skyline. Guilty as hell, of course. I'd say you're wasting time here, Sheriff. You'd better be riding after the killer. When you get him jailed, send for us. We all saw what happened to Jake."

Whereupon Sheriff Anse Crain turned wearily back to his horse and once again hoisted himself to the saddle. Hardin's voice, a taunt in it, came to him out of the darkness. "Don't forget there's a killer loose, Sheriff. You'd better polish that saddle of yours the next few days. I wouldn't want to have to go straight to the governor with a charge that you've turned too old for your job."

"I'll fetch him in!" Crain roared, nettled beyond restraint. "And I hope he makes fools out of every one of you in court!"

But he was far from confident as he rode away. He had no real desire to go chasing Melody Malone; he liked Malone and was grateful to the man for ridding Stanton City of the nuisance of Breed Lenoir. Yet there might be some grain of truth in the Quirt's story of how Jake had been killed. There'd been a great deal of town talk about the enmity between Jake and Melody Malone as a result of a pitcher of syrup; and greater tragedies had stemmed from less cause. In any case, Crain was left with his duty clear.

He had to ignore the killing of Rocky Lynch. Lynch had made a mistake in judgment and paid for it with his life, and that closed the case; for Lynch had had no business trespassing. But by the inflexibility of law, he couldn't ignore the killing of Jake. That was a horse of another colour. Yet where would a man begin looking for Melody Malone? The guitar-toting rider had had several hours start; doubtless by now the fellow was well beyond Stanton City. Come to think about it, that looked mighty bad for Malone, his running off once he'd been saved from a hangtree. The first thing to do, Anse Crain decided, was to prepare a batch of telegrams to the sheriffs of the neighbouring counties. The net would have to be spread before this night was over.

And the night was nearly gone when Crain got back to Stanton City; the false dawn was greying the east as he clambered off his jaded horse before the jail-building. His office door was open, he noticed, and somebody was inside; but Crain wasn't particularly interested. Charley, likely, or a townsman with some petty bit of trouble that couldn't wait until a decent hour. Crain faced along the boardwalk toward the railroad depot with its telegraph office.

But suddenly he was stopping in mid-stride and having a second look inside his office. It was the guitar music, reaching his ears, that transfixed him. A guitar — ? But it couldn't be! And that voice lifted in song —

"Got me a rival on Chowder Creek,
Eight feet tall in his stocking feet,
Hi, yo, diddle, di, day . . .
And this big galoot comes a-courtin' too,
All decked out like a gol-darned Sioux,

Looks like I bit off more'n I can chew,
Hi, yo, diddle, di, da-a-a-y. . . ."

Anse Crain made it back to the jail steps in one jump, and into his office with another. *"Malone!"* he cried, and Melody grinned at him. For Melody was seated in Crain's swivel chair, his feet propped upon Crain's desk, the guitar cuddled close.

"Howdy, Sheriff," he said. "Is this where a fellow turns himself in when there's a murder charge against him? I've sure gotten tired waiting for you to show up."

Chapter XI
Spade Asks A Question

Sam Weaver, riding northward on a sunlit afternoon, wore a black string tie and his best suit of clothes, garb in which he was seen only on state occasions; and the long-legged Anvil owner had also donned a solemn gravity which gave a bleakness to his usually good-humoured face. For Sam Weaver had a decision to make, and the hour had come to make it. Moreover, he had to make it alone. Events of the past forty hours had stripped him of active allies. An event of this very afternoon had given him grim reminder of the consequences of rashness. He had just come from watching the remains of Rocky Lynch lowered to a last resting place.

And so he rode now with a bit of business to transact; he was on his way to pit himself against Quirt Hardin, and the only weapon in Weaver's armament was bluff. But he could no longer delay the inevitable. His wife had made that clear to him. This very morning, when they had dressed for Lynch's funeral, she had said, "You'll finish our round-up by to-morrow night at the latest, Sam. What are you going to do then? Let those cattle stand out on the flat till they die from old age?"

Sam Weaver's wife was an exceedingly fat woman — so fat that people, seeing the two of them together, inevitably recalled the nursery rhyme about Mr. and Mrs. Jack Spratt. She possessed a boisterousness and a tremendous vitality which made her the direct opposite of her husband, and she had always been the spur which propelled Sam Weaver to action. He would have procrastinated his whole life away if it hadn't been for her, but sometimes he wished she weren't in such an infernal hurry. He'd worried enough about Quirt Hardin's scheme without having himself forced into action.

Thus he rode now with no liking for the task ahead, but with the realisation that he must return with something definite to report or there'd be the merry blue blazes to pay at home to-night. A plague on a shrewish woman! It was a choice between facing Hardin or taking a tongue-lashing, and he kept his horse headed north.

In due time he reached The Strip and followed the wire to the gate. The damage done by Lazy-L cattle the night before last had already been repaired, and Horseface Hennessey, Lazy-L's foreman, had told Weaver to-day that Hardin had permitted the Lynch crew to come inside The Strip and haze back the scattered stock. The herd stood now on their own bedding grounds on the Lazy-L, awaiting a decision which no man was as yet legally qualified to make.

At the gate, a hardcase Quirt hand wordlessly admitted Weaver, and at the far gate he was as summarily allowed to make his exit. He saw no other human between there and the Quirt buildings, but when he'd rounded the ranch-house, he found Hardin and McTeague seated upon the gallery. Weaver wondered if the two of them bunked together. With a wave of the hand from which the quirt dangled, Hardin said affably, "Howdy, Sam. Light down."

Weaver, accepting the invitation, came to the gallery and said pointedly, "I've just ridden over from the Lazy-L. Quite a turn-out to see old Rocky buried."

The heavy flesh around Hardin's eyes crinkled. "I'd like to have gone, but some folks wouldn't have thought it seemly. Believe it or not, Sam, I had nothing personal against Rocky. What's a man to do but fight when somebody sends a herd of cattle charging against his fence?"

Weaver shrugged. "You'd answer your own question one way — I another. But that gets us down to business. My cattle are about ready to trail to town."

Hardin said, "And you've come to talk it over? Alone?"

McTeague was saying nothing. He'd acknowledged Weaver's presence with a nod, no more than that. Now the gunman was busy at fashioning a cigarette, but Weaver got the feeling that McTeague was watching him, even when McTeague's eyes were upon the paper between his lean fingers. Weaver said, "I've got to act alone, now. Lynch is dead. Horseface Hennessey says Rocky has a younger brother down in Colorado somewhere. The kid brother will get the ranch, I suppose. But Otis Floren has got to locate the boy and get him up here, and that may take weeks."

"What about the C-C Connected?"

"Malone's still boss. And Malone's in jail. Gave himself up to face the charge of murdering Jake. Or so Anse Crain told me at the funeral to-day. The whole crowd was buzzing about Malone. But Dallas Spade just shrugs his shoulders now and says that he's only the foreman and can't make a move till he gets orders. That puts me on my lonesome."

"The toll," said Hardin, "is one dollar a head."

"You've got a legal right to collect toll," Weaver said patiently. "Otis Floren admits that. And you've got a legal right to defend your property. That's certainly been proved. Anse Crain isn't very happy over what happened to Rocky Lynch, but Anse told me there wasn't a thing he could do about it — not when Horseface Hennessey can't deny that your story of the ruckus is a straight story. I can't argue with you on that toll proposition. But I've talked it over with my wife, and we figure that a dollar is a little steep. We could do business at four-bits a head."

"Look, Sam, I like you," Hardin said and laid an affectionate hand on Weaver's shoulder. "You're book-learned and you're a thinking man. None of this going off half-cocked like Lynch did. That's not for you. And none of this impractical nonsense which seems to be the stock in trade of Melody Malone. I'd certainly like to cut that toll for you, Sam, but I can't do it. It wouldn't be fair, now, to lower your rate and keep the freight up for the Lazy-L and the C-C Connected, now would it?"

"I wasn't asking for a special favour," Weaver said with dignity. "In fact I wouldn't want it. I've got to live with my neighbours and look them in the eye. When I said four-bits a head, I meant four-bits for every one."

Hardin sighed a heavy sigh. "It just wouldn't be good business. There's been considerable expense connected with this matter — fetching in surveyors . . . checking the legality of my scheme . . . stringing wire . . . paying a crew fighting wages to guard it. No, sir, Sam, I couldn't do it."

"Then that leaves me with just one choice."

"To pay the dollar?"

"No," said Weaver. "To take my cattle south through the Pass of the Blackrobes and around the hills to Stanton City."

"Come now, Sam. That doesn't make sense. You know that south country as well as I do. By the time you got your beef to the railroad, they'd be so gaunted that you'd lose a lot more than a dollar when Omaha looks them over. You're not a man who'd cut off his nose to spite his face."

"This is the first season," Weaver said. "There'll be many more of them. Pay you your dollar now, and it will be two dollars next year and three the year after. No, Quirt. If there isn't any other way to buck you, I've got to take the way at hand."

Stepping down from the gallery, Weaver adjusted his sombrero, and Hardin said, "I don't like to see you losing money, Sam. Especially just to stick to a stubborn principle. And I wouldn't want us to part in anger. Tell you what, I'll shave two-bits off that toll for you, but the Lazy-L and the C-C isn't to hear about it."

An anger surged in Weaver that made him magnificent in that moment. He drew his lean body erect, and he said, "I'll be moving my cattle shortly, Quirt. If you change your mind in the meantime, send word to me that the toll is fifty cents. For everybody. Good day to you!"

Putting his back to the pair on the gallery, he headed for his horse. He heard Hardin heave another of those heavy sighs; he heard some slight movement of McTeague's that made the man's holster creak, but he didn't look back. When he'd swung to saddle and rounded the ranch-house, he still had the feeling that McTeague's eyes were upon him, and he shivered in the afternoon sun. Yet a certain pride was in him; he'd made his choice. And he'd stick to that choice. Such was the price a man had to pay for his honour. . . .

Otis Floren sat alone in his office over the mercantile store late that afternoon. He'd drawn the shade against the sunlight, and he was perched behind his desk, his eyes blank, his jaws slowly rotating as he indulged in his solitary vice; but the tobacco had no taste for him to-day. He was considering the events of the past two days and contemplating the work that had to be done — there were letters to be gotten off to Colorado — but he made no move. Some days he felt immeasurably old, and this was one of them.

Not twenty minutes before, he'd returned a rented buggy to the livery stable and come directly to his office. The town was almost deserted to-day, for there'd been two funerals, one in Stanton City's own cemetery where Jake had been laid away, the other out at the Lazy-L. That had given Floren a choice, and he'd elected to do honour to his late client. Now he was remembering his last look at Rocky Lynch, and, remembering, he sighed.

Rocky was dead. That seemed hard to grasp; there'd been so much life to the man, such a bombastic exuberance that it seemed incredible that so small a thing as a bullet could have made Rocky Lynch cold and silent. Rocky Lynch was the first casualty to have resulted from Quirt Hardin's scheme to exact toll from his neighbours. And, thinking about that, Floren wondered how much of Rocky's blood was on his own hands. He'd been Lynch's lawyer and he'd failed Lynch, just as he'd likewise failed the Anvil and the C-C

Connected. They'd turned to him when they'd sensed Hardin's scheme, and his law books had provided no weapon that could checkmate the Curling Quirt. They'd asked for advice, and he'd told them he'd hoped *they* would have the ideas.

Well, Rocky Lynch had gotten one. Rocky Lynch hadn't waited for counsel, or the co-operation of his neighbours, or any loophole that the law might have provided. Rocky Lynch had gone ahead, according to his nature, and Rocky was dead. But perhaps if Otis Floren had managed to hold out some faint hope, if he'd had an idea of his own, Rocky might have waited and been alive to-day.

Things like these always baffled Floren. The law books were his Bible, and the law was rigorous and just, but it was made to fit all men and couldn't therefore take into account that men operated each in his own fashion. There was Rocky Lynch, the bombastic, and Sam Weaver, the patient one, and Melody Malone who was something of a question mark. Floren hadn't looked into his law books when he'd gauged Malone. He'd learned that Malone had swapped away his bullets but retained his gun, and by this knowledge Floren had been inspired. A fighting man would always find bullets. Well, Malone had found them, and Jake was dead, and Malone was in jail, charged with murder. That was how good Otis Floren's guess had been.

Thinking of these things, he heard a tread upon the stairs, the beat of boots along the hall, and a rap upon the door. He rid himself of the tobacco, toed his cuspidor beneath his desk, and said, "Come in." The door opened to admit Dallas Spade. The C-C Connected foreman was wearing his best clothes again to-day, but he'd donned a black neckerchief as a concession to the occasion, and there was a certain grimness about him. He said, "Thought I'd catch you out at the Lazy-L, Floren, but you got away while I was talking to Horseface Hennessey. A bad day."

"A black day," Floren agreed.

Spade took a chair. "Reckon you've heard that Malone is in jail."

Floren nodded. "I've got to get over and see him. Crain fetched me word yesterday morning, but he likewise told me about the fight at the fence. I took the dead into consideration ahead of the living. Spent yesterday at the Lazy-L, talking to Hennessey. We looked through Rocky's papers, trying to get a line on a younger brother of Rocky's who lives down in Colorado. It was so late when we finished that Hennessey suggested I stay overnight and be on hand for the funeral to-day. I just got back to town."

"You figure Malone really beefed Jake?"

Floren frowned. "I've only got Anse Crain's story. Obviously, it's going to be mighty hard to prove that Malone didn't. The whole Quirt crew claims to have been eye-witnesses."

Spade fashioned up a cigarette and got it going. "The C-C will back Malone, Floren. You're hired as lawyer, and you can throw the whole ranch into the fight. Those are orders from Anita Corday. She sent me here to tell you that. And she said to hand this over to you. It's a note Malone left night before last when he rode away from the ranch — a note signing the C-C over to Miss Corday. She won't take the ranch, not as a gift. Says it was Chance Corday's wish that somebody else have it, and that's the way it's got to be. But she thinks this paper might help you in court. As she sees it, a man who'd give away a ranch, just on principle, isn't the kind who'd shoot down an unarmed man like Jake over a little squabble. She hopes a jury will see it the same way."

Floren took the paper, examined it carefully, and tucked it into a desk drawer. "I'll get over to the jail and have a talk with Malone," he said, coming to his feet. "And you can tell Miss Corday that I'll defend him to the best of my ability. You can also tell her that I'd have offered myself as his attorney, even if she hadn't requested it."

Spade looked at him through tobacco smoke. "You still believe in that saddle-bum, eh, Floren?"

Floren said, "And what do you think of him?"

Spade shrugged. "I've never felt that he was really the man of Chance Corday's choice. It was just a fluke of luck that made him qualify as heir. He proved that after he came out to the C-C; he wasn't much interested in how we were to cross Quirt Hardin's Strip. Yet there's something likeable about the fellow. Miss Corday wouldn't be backing him if he wasn't worth it. And I'll never believe that he killed Jake. A man like Malone would have to be pushed hard before he'd start gunning."

Floren was crossing toward the door, and Spade came to a stand, found Floren's cuspidor and dropped his cigarette into it. He cleared his throat in the manner of a man with something to say who hardly knows how to say it. "Floren, I've got something on my mind," he admitted. "Me and Chance Corday were pretty close to each other. Once he practically told me that when he was gone, the C-C Connected would be mine. Was that will you read the only one he ever wrote?"

Floren paused, a hand on the door-knob, and now it was his turn to hunt for words.

"There was another will," he admitted at last. "One that named you as heir, Spade. But when Chance wrote it, he didn't even know he had a niece, and he didn't know about this trouble that was shaping up with Quirt Hardin. When he came to me and drew up his new will — the one I read — that naturally made the earlier one null and void. Chance asked me never to mention that first will to you. He didn't want you to know he'd actually named you as heir, and then changed his mind. But you've asked me an honest question, and I've given you an honest answer."

Spade said slowly, "So that's the way it was."

"I'm sorry, son," Floren said. "It is not a pleasant experience to learn that you almost owned the C-C. I'd say that Chance provided for you handsomely."

Spade, lost in thought, recovered himself and smiled a quick smile. "I'm not complaining," he said. "Chance Corday gave me more than I had coming. But I'll always feel that the ranch should really belong to Anita. Good luck with your client, Floren. I don't want to see Malone swing for a murder he likely didn't do. But my mind is made up about one thing. The C-C Connected isn't big enough for the two of us. The day he rides back to the spread a free man, I ride away. You can tell him that, if you wish."

Chapter XII
Jailbreak

There was little about the Cinnibar County jail to encourage a man to make a lengthy stay, but Melody had managed to keep himself fairly comfortable. Fronting the log and frame building was the sheriff's office, and behind the office a long corridor ran. Giving off from this corridor were six cells, three on each side, and all of them monotonously alike. Each had a cot and blankets, likely animated, a washstand and a three-legged stool, and each had a barred window, hardly wide enough to admit the passage of a man's shoulders, even if the bars could be removed. But the main discomfort that Melody had discovered was loneliness. The county had no other customers at the moment, and Anse Crain had scarcely poked his nose into the corridor except when he fetched Melody's meals from one of the restaurants.

To all of this Melody adjusted himself with

reasonable ease. A gregarious man in spite of the lonely life of his choosing, he'd have liked company across the corridor — even if it had been some old booze-fighter who hollered in his sleep. Since there was no company, Melody amused himself in other ways. Anse Crain had allowed his prisoner to retain the silver-plated guitar, after examining it with a care that had made Melody grin. Several new verses had been added to the saga of the girl on Chowder Crick, her reluctant suitor, and his obstreperous rival. But Melody's heart wasn't completely in the composition. A change had come over Melody in these past two days, a change that had matured him.

This late afternoon he sat perched upon the stool, the guitar across his knees, his fingers idly plucking at it; but his thoughts were elsewhere, and his high-boned face had a grim cast to it. He was this way when he heard the door to the front of the building creak open, and he was instantly reminded that even though supper might be a little early, the tray would be most welcome. But it wasn't Anse Crain who came into the corridor; Melody had learned to recognise the sheriff's ponderous step. Otis Floren moved into Melody's range of vision and said, "Howdy, Malone. Couldn't find Anse about, but I presume it will be all right if I talk to you. I'm your attorney. Of my own choice, and with the backing of the C-C Connected."

Melody's face softened. "You mean Miss Corday asked you to help untangle my twine?"

Floren nodded. "We might as well get down to cases. Did you kill Jake? You can be frank with me, Malone. A killing doesn't necessarily mean a murder charge. It's the circumstances that count."

Melody shook his head. "I settled my affair with Jake the day I met him. Shucks, now, there was nothing between us that warranted a shoot-out."

"Some people might not agree," Floren said. "Crain told me the Quirt's side of it yesterday, but I've been too busy to get over here and see you. The way one of the Quirt hands gave it to Anse, Hardin and his men were patrolling the wire and heard you and Jake make loud talk. You dragged out your gun and shot Jake, and the Quirt men grabbed you. Jake had no gun, so the Quirt decided to hang you. Yesterday I heard how Dallas Spade and Anita Corday came along and cut you down. When you disappeared after that, everybody presumed you were running away. But instead you headed to town to give yourself up. Why, Malone? Most men would have really run, given the chance and with half a dozen self-styled eye-witnesses to testify against them."

Melody showed his teeth. "The better to bite Quirt Hardin with," he said.

Floren frowned in bewilderment. "You mean you think Hardin framed up this whole business? And you figured the best way to fight him would be to surrender and stand trial?"

"Something like that," Melody admitted. "I had no grudge against Hardin. I got the C-C by bucking him, but that was over and done with. I might even have decided to pay his blasted toll when the time came to move the C-C cattle. But all that's changed. The deal has gotten personal now. Did you ever sit on a horse, Floren, with a hang-rope around your neck and your hands tied behind you, knowing that when the horse moved, you'd start kicking out your life on thin air? It's a mighty provoking situation to be in. It don't make you kindly toward the gent that dreamed up the idea. I'm fighting Hardin from here on out. But the first thing to do is stand trial on this murder business and clear myself. Hardin thought I'd hang, and, when that didn't work, he probably figured I'd cut and run. That makes two surprises he's gotten so far."

Floren gave all this due consideration,

absent-mindedly reaching for his tobacco plug as he did. Discovering it in his hand, he coloured and extended the plug toward Melody; but Melody shook his head. "One habit I never got, mister. It would have interfered with business. Used to be I had a harmonica rigged up on a wire frame and played it along with my guitar."

Floren reached into the breast pocket of his coat and found a cigar which he thrust between the bars. "Try one of these, then."

Melody ran his nose the length of the cigar, and his face lighted, but he pocketed the weed. A cigar, he decided, would taste good after supper.

Floren, self-exposed, worried off a corner of the tobacco plug. "I think I can put the pieces together now," he said. "The Quirt bunch framed up this murder story, and they all intend to swear to it. That will make it your word against theirs on the witness stand. I'll try to get a change of venue, but likely it won't be granted, and you'll be tried here in Stanton City. Which means that every man on the jury will be remembering that a verdict in your favour will be the same as calling Hardin and McTeague and those others liars. We'll be hard put to get a jury that long on nerve. Out best hope is the judge, who'll be an outsider. But even then the evidence will be against you."

"Evidence? What evidence?"

"The circumstances, Malone. Jake sent you up against Breed Lenoir the first day you were here, just as a joke. That bit of horseplay might have cost you your hide. Some men would have gone gunning for Jake right then and there. Instead, you poured a pitcher of syrup into his pants, and slapped his face — acts that made Jake your enemy for life. You'd turned him into a laughing stock, and Jake was the kind whose sense of humour worked only one way. He threatened you with a meat cleaver after that, and when you got around to restocking your cartridge belt, the whole town rather expected there might be fireworks between the two of you. But shortly after, you moved out to the C-C Connected."

"Which should make a jury think twice about whether I was hankering for Jake's scalp."

"But Jake might have taken up from there. Or so a jury could reason. He was very cantankerous after that affair in his restaurant; nobody ordered syrup for their flapjacks without getting a scowl from Jake. Supposing Jake had taken it into his head to ride out to the C-C and challenge you to meet him there in Stanton to settle the matter? That's the way Jake might have wanted it — a fight on the main street so he could restore his prestige. And supposing Jake didn't have to ride all the way to the ranch because he met you heading north that night? Jake challenged you to a fight; you laughed at him, and that made Jake all the angrier. The talk got mighty colourful. Then Jake might have reached for a handkerchief, or made some sort of gesture toward a pocket. You thought he was going for a gun, so you fired. The Quirt man who fetched Jake's body to town gave Crain your gun. One bullet was gone."

"McTeague fired that bullet."

"Of course," Floren said. "But the picture I've just painted is the one the jury will see after Hardin's crew has testified. Your only chance is that they'll let you off easy on the grounds that you thought you were defending yourself. But that isn't likely. They'll argue that you should have been sure Jake was armed before you got your gun to going."

"Hardin's bunch had Jake's body with them when they found me near the fence," Melody said. "From the talk they made, I gathered that they knew I'd been at the C-C ranchhouse, and they were figuring on toting the body there. Finding me on the road was pure luck, but that meant they had to make up a new story, and Hardin spun one right then and there, and told his crew to be sure and get it straight. Hardin didn't mind my listening, too. He figured I'd shortly be dead, and even if I lived he could always make a liar out of me. It would be my story against his."

"And that's still the size of it, Malone."

"Except for one thing. *Why did Hardin kill Jake?*"

"That's simple enough. To frame you. Hardin lost stature on this range when you defied him that first day and won yourself a ranch. More than that, he's probably been afraid that the south ranchers would look to the C-C for leadership, as in the past, and the new C-C boss, a man who'd already bucked him, was therefore a menace. Hardin has doubtless been scheming all along to get you out of the way, Malone."

"So he found Jake riding out on the range, figured that Jake, dead, would make a murder charge that could be saddled on to me, and shot him?" Melody shook his head. "That would have been too risky. Hardin would have had a corpse on his hands and a lot of ifs and buts between beefing Jake and hanging the job on to me. My guess is that Hardin had his own reasons for killing Jake. After the job was done, he needed a goat, and I'm the gent who qualified."

Floren stroked his chin thoughtfully. "Perhaps you've struck it!" he announced, excitement in his voice. "At least you've put your finger on our one hope. Prove that Hardin killed Jake, and you've automatically proved that you *didn't*. But how?"

"That's what I've been wondering," Melody admitted ruefully. "I worked the thing out in my mind after I'd surrendered. I wish now I hadn't been so quick at giving myself up. Outside, I might stand a chance at tangling Hardin's twine. Do you think you could peel this pokey off me?"

Floren shook his head. "A habeas corpus wouldn't stick on a murder charge, and, according to the coroner's verdict, Jake was murdered. But I'm going to get to work on your idea."

A new thought, striking Floren, made him glance nervously over his shoulder and along the jail corridor. "I don't like Crain's leaving you here alone," he said. "I've just now realised how dangerous it is. Hardin is sly, and Hardin may guess that sooner or later you were bound to get to wondering just why Jake did die. Therefore Hardin would sooner have you dead than brought to trial. With you out of the picture, the case is closed. Watch yourself, boy. I'm going to have Crain keep a jailer here. He can swear in a temporary deputy."

Melody crossed over to the cot and seated himself upon it. "Talk to me, Floren," he said. "All I'll be able to do in here is think, but

I want fuel for the fire. Tell me all you can about Jake and about Hardin, yes, and about anybody else who comes to your mind. I want the whole picture of this Cinnibar range and its people. Maybe somewhere in your talk, I'll find some pieces to fit together."

Floren, leaning against the bars, obeyed. He told of Jake's coming to Stanton City, and everything else that crossed his mind concerning the restaurant man. He spoke of Hardin's arrival, too, and the man's rise to power. That led him to Chance Corday and Rocky Lynch and Sam Weaver and Dallas Spade, and he sketched word pictures of these men, Melody listening the while and occasionally asking a question. An hour ran on, and another, and Floren became hoarse. But Melody had made a good listener. Floren said then, "I'll be getting along now. You'll see me whenever I've time to drop in."

After the lawyer had gone, Melody soon became acutely aware that it was long past supper time and that he was ravenously hungry. Darkness had settled upon the Cinnibar; Melody, crossing to the little barred window, could see a sweep of stars overhead and glimpse some of the buildings along the main street, but there was no sign of the familiar bulk of Sheriff Anse Crain. Half an hour later the sheriff came in. He'd fetched food, and he set the tray down in the corridor while he fumbled with his keys. Once the tray was moved inside the cell, Crain lighted the smoky lamp which was suspended in the corridor.

"Plumb sorry to be so slow getting over here with your grub," Crain apologised. "Had a little work to do that tied me up. This is the only job in the county that keeps a man goin' twenty-six hours out of every twenty-four."

Melody was more interested in the food than in the conversation, but he said, "Somebody steal a horse, Sheriff?"

Crain shook his head. "The mercantile store got broken into. Sully Meek closed up this afternoon so he could go out to Rocky Lynch's funeral, and he got back so late he decided there was no sense in opening. But a little after dark he went into the store, figgering he'd work on his accounts for a while. Found the padlock had been twisted off the back door and somebody had got in. He came after me then. I was having my own supper and thinking about getting yours at the time."

"This Sully Meek fellow lose much?"

"That's the funny part of it," Crain said. "So far as he could figger, the only thing that was taken was a couple of cases of dynamite, some fuse and caps. Sully keeps the stuff in stock for the prospectors who range the

Cinnibar Hills, and for anybody who wants to hoist a stump in a hurry. I cut for sign, and it looked like there might have been fresh wagon tracks out behind the store, but I couldn't be sure. Now I've got to go out and ride me some wide circles on the off chance that I'll run into the thieves. If I don't get back to-night, I'll pick up the tray in the morning. So long, feller." Melody gave him a wave of his hand, his mouth being too full for a proper adieu. He heard Crain's boots thump along the corridor, heard doors open and close, but he'd forgotten the sheriff by the time he'd finished the meal. The tray set aside, Melody was shaping up a cigarette when he remembered the cigar Floren had given him. Fumbling for the weed, he got it to burning and arose and stretched himself luxuriously. That lamp out in the corridor threw little light, the cell was almost lost in the shadows, and Melody, properly fed, had a feeling of aloneness and comfort.

Until he got two or three good drags on the cigar. It had obviously lingered in Floren's pocket a long time, and its odour had been a snare and a delusion, for it was far from tasty. Crossing to the window, Melody looked out, wondering if Anse Crain were yet up into the saddle and off on his lonely and, likely, futile ride. He drew upon the cigar, found it even more distasteful, and, with a wry grimace, placed it upon the window-sill, the glowing butt pointed outward, and stepped towards his guitar which stood leaning against the stool.

Afterwards, he was willing to swear that he felt the air-lash of the bullet, it was that close, but everything that happened to Melody in the next moment was pure instinct on his part. He heard the roar of the gun, off yonder in the darkness beyond the jail building, but by then he was flattened on the floor and hugging close to it. Somebody had fired through the open window, and fired so accurately that the cigar came tumbling to the floor and rolled near Melody's hand. The bullet had passed through the cell, found its way between the bars of the door, which were in line with the window, and likely that chunk of lead was embedded in the wall of the cell across the corridor.

Melody cautiously raised his head, came then to a stand, and edged toward the window. Out yonder someone was yelling hoarsely. That was Anse Crain's voice; the sheriff hadn't yet quit the town. Melody glimpsed dim movement, and for an instant saw a mounted man wheeling his saddler off into the deeper darkness. Hooves beat along an alleyway; the sheriff's voice lifted again, and the sheriff's gun spoke, but there was never a falter in the beat of those hooves. Melody tried to get a glimpse of the lawman, but apparently Crain had been out in front of the building when the bushwhacker had made his attempt, and Crain was still beyond Melody's range of vision.

But Crain was coming into the building now; Melody heard the door bang open. And in that instant Melody made a decision. A lot had raced through his mind since the moment when he realised that the bullet had been intended for him, and none of his thoughts had been pleasant. The would-be killer had seen the glowing end of the cigar and supposed that Melody had been standing at the window to do his smoking — and that had been true until Melody had placed the cigar on the sill. Old Lady Luck had certainly had her arms around him then! His single glimpse of the bushwhacker had shown him a man of the cut of McTeague — though he couldn't be sure about that. But he was remembering Floren's fear now, and he was also remembering that where a first attempt at killing him had failed, a second might likely succeed.

And that was why he realised so readily that he must get himself out of this jail. Surrendering to the law had proved to be a mistake from any viewpoint. And so, with Crain hurrying into the corridor, Melody silently slumped to the floor and assumed a sprawling position, his back to the planking. There was a way of turning near-disaster into opportunity, and he'd seen the way. Crain, fumbling frantically with his keys, was crying, "Did they get you, feller?" The door swung inward, and Crain was bending over him, one knee to the floor.

Melody did two things then, so quickly that they blended into a single act. His right hand raised to Crain's holster and snatched the sheriff's gun from it. Bringing up the gun, Melody sent its barrel smashing between Crain's eyes. Without a groan, Crain collapsed across him, unconscious, and Melody had to drag himself from beneath the man's inert body.

Getting to a stand, Melody looked down upon the fallen man, not liking this thing he had had to do, but realising that he'd just forged a more effective habeas corpus than any Otis Floren could produce. He wanted the sheriff held here for a while, and his first thought was to pick up Crain's keys and leave the sheriff locked in this cell. But he quickly changed his mind about that. The killer might come back this very night, and if the killer ventured to look through the window, he might mistake Crain for Melody Malone. So

Melody toiled at dragging Crain out through the open doorway and along the corridor and into the office.

Here he found a pair of handcuffs in Crain's desk, and he slipped them on the man. Likewise he gagged Crain with the sheriff's own neckerchief, for Crain was already stirring. Another pair of handcuffs fastened the sheriff's ankles, once Melody had peeled the boots from the man. The keys to the cuffs tossed into a corner, Melody gazed upon his handiwork with what little satisfaction he could get from thus dealing with a man to whom he had owed no hurt, and whom he rather liked.

"Plumb sorry, feller," he whispered and prepared to leave. Just how long it would be before someone found Crain here and managed to release the sheriff was a matter of conjecture. But this Melody knew. He'd have to make the time count. For his chore now was to pin the killing of Jake upon Quirt Hardin, and, however that task was to be accomplished, it must be done before the law got into action again.

Chapter XIII
The Shape of Disaster

Melody finding his gun and belt in Anse Crain's desk, helped himself to these articles. Also, he took his guitar from the cell and slung it across his back. He was fully aware that the instrument would readily identify him, even from a distance, but he would have felt naked without it. Casting one last glance about the sheriff's office, he eased Crain's inert form into a more comfortable position, then quietly slipped from the building.

Stanton City looked deserted to-night. With two funerals to turn the populace to sober reflection, there were few horses at the hitchrails of the various saloons, and no roistering riders to stir the dust of the main street. Whoever had broken into Sully Meek's mercantile store had picked a good night for such depredation. Even the shooting by the bushwhacker and Sheriff Crain had failed to bring any loiterers on the run. But Melody was acutely mindful that the would-be assassin might still be about, and he almost regretted fetching along his guitar. Hugging close to the buildings, he soon eased between two of them and made his way to the alley. Here he moved cautiously, trying to remember the street as it had looked from the boardwalk. He had a destination in mind, but now he was proceeding with little more than instinct to guide him.

Jake's Eating Place, as observed from the street, had appeared to be dark. With Jake's funeral held not many hours before, Mrs. Jake had doubtless closed the restaurant to-day. But as Melody felt his way along the alley, he soon discovered that light glowed in the rear of the building, and he judged that Jake's living quarters had been here, adjacent to the kitchen. He almost stumbled over a garbage barrel as he approached the place, and something streaked past him in the Stygian darkness, brushing against his leg. Lamplight from a rear window, reflecting, made a livid green spot in the darkness as the nocturnal creature turned. Melody breathed a gusty sigh of relief.

"Brutus, you old son-of-a-gun," he said softly. By grab, his nerves had gotten jumpy!

The one-eyed tom-cat made soft movement in the darkness and was gone. Melody fumbled toward the rear door of the restaurant building, then paused, listening intently. A faint stirring within, but there was no talk, which meant, as near as he could judge, that whoever was inside was alone. He raised his knuckles and tapped lightly, and in a moment the door was thrown open and Mrs. Jake stood there.

She didn't recognise him in that first instant. Her eyes had not adjusted themselves to the darkness, and he took advantage of this to say quickly, "Please let me in. It's important."

Something in his tone must have been as reassuring as it was urgent, for she stepped aside, a gesture of her head bidding him enter. She was wearing a black dress which made her more shapeless than ever, but she didn't look as though she'd spent much time at weeping. Melody bobbed inside, closed the door and put his back to it. Mrs. Jake said listlessly, "So it's you." Then, with a slightly greater show of interest: "Thought you was in jail?"

"I broke out," Melody admitted. "I want to talk to you. But before I do, there's one thing you've got to get straight. I didn't kill Jake, ma'am."

She slumped into a rocker. "Any fool could tell that," she said. "If you'd been set on a killing, you'd have dusted off Jake that first day you were here."

"What did Jake go to see Quirt Hardin about the day Jake died?"

Her eyes quickly lifted, and suspicion was

in them. "How'd you know Jake went to the Curling Quirt?"

"I didn't," Melody admitted. "I was just guessing. But now you've told me that I guessed right. What *did* he go about?"

Her mouth drew tight. "I ain't doin' no talkin'," she said firmly.

"Look," Melody pleaded. "You might say I'm here to help you, though it's my own hide that's got me the most interested. I never killed Jake, but I've got pretty good reason to guess that Quirt Hardin did. Him, or one of his hands. They rigged that killing so it would look pretty on me, and I gave myself up to the law to stand trial and try to prove them wrong. But I've decided since that I can do more good for myself outside those bars. My chore is to pin that killing right back on to Hardin. You want to see the man who killed Jake hang for it, don't you? Then that puts us in the same boat."

Mrs. Jake said, "Hardin hasn't taken to killing women. Not yet. But he'd see me dead before he'd see his own neck in a hangnoose. What have I got to gain?"

"Nothing — if you look at it that way," Melody said, and, turning, he put his hand on the doorknob.

The woman said, "Just a minute. Maybe you're right. Jake wasn't much good to anybody — not even to himself. But he was my man. What is it you want to know?"

"Why he went to the Quirt the other day."

"He didn't say. He dressed himself up in his best and made a lot of foolish talk about getting Quirt Hardin to share his wealth with him. Tried to make believe he knew something about Hardin that would make Hardin willing to pay. He hinted that it had to do with Hardin shooting at Brutus that first day you were in town."

"Brutus? The tom-cat?"

The woman nodded. "That was about all Jake said. He rented a horse from the livery stable and lit out. I never saw him alive again."

Melody's high-boned face crinkled with thought. "Everybody on the street saw Hardin shoot at the cat that day," he mused. "Now what was there about that deal that made Jake think he could squeeze money out of Hardin just because he saw it too?"

Mrs. Jake shook her head. "I dunno. I've been thinking about it too. Maybe Jake tied up that deal in his mind with the time Hardin come and got Brutus."

"You mean that Hardin came to town after the cat?"

"Weeks ago. Brutus don't belong to nobody, but he hangs out behind the restaurant a lot. Eats scraps. Jake and me was toting the barrel out one night, and we found Hardin putting the cat in a gunny-sack. Said he figured he'd give Brutus a home on the Curling Quirt, there being a lot of mice in the barn. We didn't give him no argument; he had as much right as anybody to help himself to the cat. Then he asked us if we'd wrap up some fish for the cat. Everybody knows that Brutus is crazy about fish. But that struck me as kind of funny. Quirt Hardin ain't one for throwing his change around. If he had so many mice he needed a cat on place, why was he spoiling the cat with fish?"

"It makes no sense," Melody conceded.

"That's about as much as I can tell you, mister. Nobody saw Brutus again until that day you fetched him into town."

"I found him walking across the prairie. He was stalking a gopher, but he gave that up when I came along. I saw he was headed for town, so I gave him a lift. Cats have a habit of coming back from wherever they're taken, even if it's a good many miles. Maybe Brutus didn't like it on the Curling Quirt and got to pining for the garbage barrel out back of here. But why did Hardin take a shot at him?"

The woman shrugged. "You tell me," she said. "Whatever the answer is, Jake guessed at it and thought his guess was good enough to blackmail Hardin. Sort of looks like something happened while Hardin had the cat that Hardin would just as soon was forgotten."

Melody lost himself in thought again. "A jury would jug us for life if we started talking about cats and fish on the witness stand," he said. "But thanks a heap, anyway. All I'm doing is collecting pieces. Patched together, all they make is a crazy quilt. Now think back just once more. What happened on this range during the time Brutus was at the Curling Quirt?"

The woman's face showed her effort at recollection. "Nothing much," she finally decided. "Not that Brutus could have had something to do with anyway. Oh, yes, it was during that time that the C-C Connected ranch-house had its fire and Chance Corday got himself burned to death."

For a moment Melody showed no real interest in this piece of information, and then, suddenly, he was rigid with attention. "I'll be going now," he said quickly. "Maybe I've got a heap to thank you for. Time will tell. I've got a crazy notion, but if it's right, you've told me what it was that Jake guessed. So long."

His excitement was contagious enough to arouse the slatternly woman, but he closed the door on her startled questions and was off down the alley. Bobbing between two buildings, he risked crossing the street, and in this manner he came to the ravaged mercantile store. But his eyes were lifted upward as he angled across to the building, lifted to the second story where Otis Floren maintained his living quarters as well as his office.

Floren's bedroom was dark, but its window was just above the wooden awning that fronted the mercantile and shaded its porch. With a quick look to left and right to be sure that no wayfarers were in sight, Melody shinnied up a support and pulled himself on to the sloping roof of the awning. His knuckles drummed lightly on the partially raised window, and in a few moments he heard the sleepy voice of Otis Floren.

"What is it?" the lawyer demanded.

"Come here a minute," Melody whispered.

A rustling of blankets . . . the padding of bare feet upon the floor . . . a low ejaculation as Floren stumbled against a chair in the darkness. Then the sash was raised and the lawyer peered out, a nightcap perched upon his head.

"*Malone!*" ejaculated. "What in the name of sanity are you doing out of jail?"

"Shhh!" Melody cautioned him. "I wrote out my own habeas corpus. You were right about that jail being mighty unhealthy. Hear a commotion a while ago? Somebody took a shot at me through the window. That was when I decided to vacate. Anse Crain came rushing in to see whether I'd been perforated. I slugged him with his own gun."

Floren shook his head dazedly. "That's not going to help your case any," he muttered.

"The next time I see Anse Crain, I want to be able to send him chasing somebody else besides me. And I've been working on the case. Tell me this, Floren: Just exactly *what* caused Chance Corday to die?"

"Why, he was burned to death, of course. You've seen the ranch-house. Chance was trapped in that fire."

"But are you *sure* nothing happened to him before the fire got him? A crushed skull, for instance? Or a bullet through his heart? Maybe the fire was just to cover up the real thing."

"Now what in the world ever gave you that idea?" Floren demanded, but the lawyer had been impressed. "I couldn't say for sure. What was left of Chance wasn't pretty. We got him into a coffin as quickly as possible, and we held the funeral with a sealed coffin. There was an inquest, but it was only a formality. That gutted ranch-house was evidence enough as to what had happened to Chance."

"Got a sawbones in this town?" Melody inquired. "Somebody who's qualified to give Chance's body a real going over and able to tell afterwards exactly what killed him?"

"Of course," Floren said. "Doc Bishop. But do you think that's really necessary and advisable? We'd have to open the grave. I'm not sure just what legal procedure —"

"To blazes with legal procedure!" Melody interjected quickly. "You get that grave open and let the sawbones have his look. I've got to lay low, but I'll get back to you as soon as possible and find out what the doc reported. There's no time now for windy talking; Anse Crain is on ice, but maybe not for long. But here's my guess, Floren: Chance Corday didn't die in an accident. He was murdered. And there's only one man on Cinnibar Range who had reason for wanting Corday six feet under. Quirt Hardin. Remembering all that palavering you did in the jail about the folks on this range? Hardin feared Corday because Chance was bound to be the leader of the south range ranchers when they opposed Hardin's scheme."

"Chance — murdered!" Floren shook his head.

"That's my hunch. And Jake made a pretty close guess as to who murdered him — and how. So Jake had to die, too. But Hardin aimed on making that second killing do double duty. He was going to get rid of me by making me out to be Jake's murderer."

Floren was like a man in a trance. "I'll have

Doc Bishop out to the C-C to-morrow," he promised. "I've got to ride that way myself. Sam Weaver sent one of his boys into town this evening to tell me that the Anvil has decided to head its cattle south. I'm going to try talking Sam into waiting until the Anvil and the C-C can act together. It's a pity Sam didn't learn through Lynch's mistake that nothing's gained by acting alone. Taking the back door out of the Cinnibar is going to run all the tallow off Sam's cattle. And I'm not sure he'll be avoiding trouble, either. Supposing Hardin tries keeping Weaver from going through the pass?"

"You mean Hardin might slam the back door in Weaver's face?" Melody asked, and something in his own question gave him its answer and a sudden glimpse of the shape of disaster. "Of course!" he added. "That's exactly what Hardin's going to do! Floren, somebody broke into the store tonight and took two cases of dynamite! That made no sense to Anse Crain. Nor to me, at the time. Hardin's work! He's going to blow the pass shut. But supposing Weaver is putting his cattle through at that very time!"

Floren reeled slightly. "And you put the sheriff out of commission!" he groaned. "Who's going to stop Hardin now?"

"I am!" Melody declared, and he was lowering himself over the edge of the porch as he spoke. Clinging only with his hands, he swung his body outward and released his grip. And he lighted running.

Chapter XIV
Pass of the Blackrobes

Melody's horse had been impounded at the livery stable by the sheriff's order at the time Melody had surrendered to the law. Thus, after leaving Otis Floren, Melody headed directly to the stable and was comforted to find the place deserted. The hostler was out for the moment, but the door gave to Melody's touch, and he groped in the darkness for his saddle and other gear. These in his hands, he fell to saddling his horse; and the mount, weary of confinement, whinnied eagerly.

"Shhh!" Melody cautioned. "I'm busting you out of jail!"

A few minutes later he was walking the mount along Stanton City's main street, and then he was crossing the tangle of railroad tracks and sidings where the empty shipping pens stood in stark silhouette. Heading south at a steady lope, he rode as cautiously as his desperate urgency permitted, keeping off the wagon road and striking directly overland. He was a fugitive now, and therefore fair prey for any man's gun, and there was the remembrance of that fellow who'd fired at him through the cell window to-night. As a roving minstrel, he'd craved the public eye; but being a celebrity had backfired.

He met no other horseman on that long night's riding. The Cinnibar lay swathed in darkness, the hills bulking dimly in the distance, and the miles unreeled monotonously. Reaching The Strip at a considerable distance from the gate, he merely lifted on the reins, and his horse, eager to stretch its legs, cleared the wire with inches to spare. Melody repeated this performance at the south fence, saw the gnarled cottonwood where he'd nearly forfeited his life to Quirt Hardin's scheming, and, orienting himself by this landmark, he lined out for the C-C.

Reaching the road, he took to it now and passed the fork which branched off toward the Anvil and the Lazy-L, and he came within the hour to where the buildings of the C-C sprawled. Melody could only guess at the time, for the sky was too overcast to give him a real look at the cowboy's clock — the stars — but he judged that it was near midnight. But a light burned in the ranch-house, and that gave him pause. Anita might be up, which was all very well, but if she had visitors — neighbours who'd returned with her after Rocky Lynch's funeral to-day — those visitors might react most unhappily to the sight of a man who was presumably in jail on a murder charge. Skirting the house carefully, he saw no alien buckboard in the yard, no strange saddlers turned loose in the corrals. Satisfied, he dismounted and tramped to the door.

Anita answered his knock, but behind her loomed Dallas Spade, the naked gun in Spade's hand making mute testimony to the tension that had taken hold of the Cinnibar's people. Anita said, *"You — !"* breathlessly, and Spade cased his gun as Melody stepped inside. "I know you're both surprised to see me," Melody said quickly. "I haven't time for questions. I busted out of jail to-night because somebody had sized me up as a clay pigeon in a shooting gallery. I'm heading to the Pass of the Blackrobes as fast as I can ride. Somebody took dynamite from the mercantile to-night, and Sam Weaver aims on taking his cattle through the pass."

Spade's lean face stiffened. "You figure Hardin's closing the pass?"

"I'm going on guesswork," Melody admitted. "But for what other purpose would anybody *steal* dynamite? The stuff is cheap enough to buy, if they'd wanted it for a legitimate reason. No, whoever ran off with those overgrown firecrackers intends putting them to a use that won't stand the light of day. And when I heard that Sam Weaver was trailing south, that seemed to be the answer."

Spade said grimly, "Then I'm riding south with you. One man can't stop Hardin's bunch."

Melody shook his head. "Hardin won't send his whole crew for that job. He wouldn't dare. Somebody might get the notion to claw down his fence meanwhile. Two or three of his boys can likely take care of that blasting job. And the man who stops them will have to move careful. The more of us that head south, the more likely we'll be to tip our hand. I'm going alone."

Spade frowned. "That an order? You're still the boss, I reckon."

Melody said, "To-day Floren told me about Corday's *first* will, Spade. Is that why you always give off sparks whenever I come up against you? Call it an order, if you like. It's just plain hoss sense, as far as I'm concerned. And there's work for you, too. Head over to Sam Weaver's and tell him what's up. He might just as well start driving his cattle south anyway. He can't leave his gather standing while I'm playing out a hunch. About how far is it to the pass?"

"Fifteen miles or so, Malone."

"A good day's driving with cattle. If Weaver gets started in the morning, he'll be hitting the pass just about sundown. By that time the trail will either be closed, or I'll have put the Injun sign on Hardin's blasters. Tell Weaver to come along with his ears perked and his eyes sharpened. I'll be watching for the herd."

"I'll do more than tell Weaver," Spade promised. "I'll be with him. If there's going to be trouble at the pass, I'm going to be in on it."

Melody stepped toward the door, and Anita, who'd stood silently listening to all this, seized his arm. "Wait," she cried. "I'll put up some food for you. You may be in the hills a long time."

He nodded, and when Anita had left the room, Spade regarded Melody curiously and said, "Every time I get you written down in my tally book for what I think you are, mister, you fool me. There wasn't ten cents worth of fight in you between the day you dusted off Breed Lenoir and the last time I saw you, with your neck in a noose. Now you're itching to bite off a chunk of trouble on your lonesome. Maybe you're right about one man cutting sign on those dynamiters a lot easier than two. But what made you decide to be that one man?"

Melody shrugged. "This is one time the law could step in on Hardin. But I left the jail too fast to be polite, and I had to use the sheriff pretty rough. That makes it my job to do his work. Besides, Hardin made it a personal deal when he put a rope around my neck. I've bought in for keeps, Spade."

C-C's foreman expelled a gusty sigh. "I'll go saddle you a fresh cayuse. You'll want to hit the pass while you've still got darkness to cover you, and that will take tall riding. I wish you knew this country better. Straight south will bring you to the pass. It's really a rocky canyon, snaking between the hills. It's walls are steep and high in places, and there's a rim on either side. Hardin's boys will likely climb to one of the rims and plant the stuff in a crevice. Two cases of dynamite will drop quite a few tons of rock into the canyon. Watch for sign when you get there. Your problem will be to guess which rim they'll choose. I'll go rig up a horse for you now."

"Better not," Melody advised. "My own cayuse has got plenty of miles left in him, and I shouldn't be surprised but what Anse Crain will be paying this spread a visit, come tomorrow. He'll be in a bad frame of mind, the sheriff will. If he finds my cayuse here, he might jail the whole C-C outfit for aiding and abetting me."

Spade smiled. "If he does, we'll swear you swapped cayuses in the dead of night. He can't tack horse-stealing on to you — not when you own the C-C."

Melody followed the man out of the house and to the corrals, and, when a leggy saddler was ready for him, Anita shaped up out of the shadows and handed a saddle-bag to Melody. "Be careful," she said, her concern so genuine that it was warming. Melody caught Spade's glance and found it dark, and he knew that Spade, too, had sensed Anita's worry. Wordlessly, Melody swung to the saddle, waved his hand, wheeled the horse and aimed it south. Spade cupped his hands to his mouth and shouted, "Hey! What's the idea of toting your guitar along?" But Melody was already loping away.

To the south of the C-C Connected was indeed unfamiliar country, and Melody wished for moonlight before he'd put many miles behind him. But at least he couldn't go astray, for he had only to keep his eyes on the bulking Cinnibars and to head to where they pinched together. But no matter how much distance he put behind him, it seemed as though the hills came no closer. The country grew increasingly rougher; he lost sight of the Cinnibars as lesser hills crowded around him, and he began to wish he'd heeded Dallas Spade and fetched the foreman along. He became conscious that the land was gradually tilting upward; clumps of bushes and trees began to loom darkly, the footing was strewn with rocks, and he had to hold his horse to a walk.

An hour of this and he was leading the mount and picking a careful way through a country that had become a nightmare. Even by daylight this was no land for easy traversing, and he could understand why the south Cinnibar ranchers had considered the Pass of the Blackrobes only as a last resort in beating Hardin's scheme. A man could count on losing a good many cattle through broken legs while trolling into the hills. And when the darkness before dawn began pressing down upon the Cinnibar, Melody had to trust largely to instinct as he groped carefully forward.

The dawn came at long last, lining the eastern hills in a glory of scarlet and gold, and the light spread down to the range and gave contour and hue to the rugged country. A great weariness in Melody attested to the many miles he'd covered, but at least the going was now easier, and that thought reinvigorated him. And soon thereafter he saw the pass.

To his left a hogback had reared itself, and Melody had dismounted, leaving his weary cayuse with reins trailing, and clambered to the top of this ridge. Flattened out, he peered from this vantage point and glimpsed the rough slot in the hills, the entrance to the walled ravine that was the back door to the Cinnibar. Here was the pass that ancient zealots had discovered and given the Indian name for the Jesuits — the Blackrobes; here was long trail's ending. But there was no sign of any other humans, and Melody descended laboriously to his horse.

Now came the job of cutting for signs on Hardin's men, but there was no place to commence. On either side of the pass the ground sloped upward to the rim, and, if Spade's theory was correct, anyone who had preceeded Melody here had probably climbed one of those slopes or the other. But which one? And now that he'd reached his destination, Melody began to wonder if the wild hunch that had fetched him here had been wrong. Where was the proof that it had been Quirt hands who'd helped themselves to Sully Meek's stock? Perhaps some down-on-his-luck prospector had staked himself to a fresh try by breaking into the store and taking the dynamite.

So thinking, Melody mounted and rode aimlessly forward. Sometimes he paused and listened; sound should carry far at this altitude, but he heard only the ordinary noises of a woods awakened. And then, in a clump of trees near the base of the right hand slope, he found a wagon. It was a light wagon, and it stood deserted back here in the timber; and at the moment Melody spied it, his horse nickered all too loudly. Melody came down out of the saddle with a gun in his hand, but the silence, restored, held to its customary hush. Edging forward, Melody caught the sheen of the early light upon moving horses, and, parting a clump of bushes, he saw a hobbled team, unharnessed and grazing. But now he sucked in his breath triumphantly, for those horses bore the Curling Quirt brand.

Here was a telling picture to be read, and the sign could be put together with reasonable accuracy. Quirt hands had indeed come to this vicinity, and they'd needed a wagon on their trek — needed it because they'd been carrying something too bulky to be conveniently mounted behind a saddle. The stolen dynamite — ? Likely. They'd come this far, and they could come no farther, so they'd concealed the wagon back here in the trees, safe from the eyes of the Anvil crew who would shortly be heading this way with a trail herd. And, since the wagon was empty, that meant they'd gone on, carrying the dynamite with them.

And now Melody's search was narrowed, for obviously the Quirt hands had ascended the slope ahead — the slope which brought a man to the right hand rim of the canyon snaking through the hills. Hardin's men would have fetched the wagon as near to their destination as possible, and the finding of the wagon indicated the slope of their choice. Melody began looking for tracks now. The ground was rocky, but there was sign enough. Two men had alighted from the wagon and headed in the direction of the slope.

Lifting his eyes to that tilting ascent, Melody reached a decision. He led his horse deeper into the brush and to a considerable distance from the Quirt wagon, and here he loosened the saddle girth and then tied the mount to a tree. Threading his way back to the slope, he began climbing it. A stiffish ascent, and the guitar, bouncing against his back, reminded him that he was still carrying the instrument. He wished that he'd cached it near where he'd left his horse, but he didn't want to waste the time making a second trip; and this slope was too bald to leave the guitar lying.

The crest attained he began following along the rim of the canyon. Brush grew to the lip of the ravine in many places, huge boulders strewed this comparatively level table-land, and sometimes he could look down into the canyon, and sometimes he had to veer far away from the rim. He was hurrying as fast as he dared, spurred by the certainty that Hardin's men were indeed here and might at this very moment be preparing an explosion which would close the canyon. But time and again he paused, listening intently for the sound of voices or footfalls. None reached him.

A litter of rocks blocked the way, and he began working through it, sometimes falling to his hands and knees to clamber around a misshapen obstruction. The sun was now high enough to make him sweat, and before he'd ventured far into this maze, he had to pause to catch his breath. Taking the guitar from his back, he placed it beside him and squatted in the shadow of a rock which stood as high as a man's waist. He was beginning to feel the need for sleep, and though he promised himself he'd linger here only for a moment, perhaps he dozed. The scrape of a bootsole brought him abruptly awake. He would have come to his feet then, but a voice arrested him. It was McTeague speaking, and McTeague said, "Keep your hand away from your gun, mister!"

The gunman was standing upon the rounded top of a boulder not six feet away from Melody, and McTeague had a six-shooter in his hand. His mummy face as inscrutable as always, McTeague said, "A flown jailbird, eh?" And cocked the six-shooter. "They're always in season. I missed last night, through your cell window. But that was last night. Your luck's run out, Malone."

And this, Melody knew, was the pronouncement of his doom.

Chapter XV
Dynamite!

Here was the picture Melody would likely carry into eternity with him: McTeague standing atop the boulder, his tall, lean, black-clad form in stark silhouette, the gun rigid in his hand, the man's face showing neither exultation nor regret; but only the graven inflexibility of a man without feeling. McTeague held all the cards, and they were in his right hand. McTeague wouldn't have to answer for killing an escaped prisoner.

Whereupon Melody said desperately, "The shot you fire is going to fetch about five of the C-C boys on the run."

"You're a liar," McTeague said without rancour. "My job was to watch the back trail. You came alone."

Hidden in McTeague's words was information — providing Melody could live to use it. Two Quirt hands had come here. Apparently, then, the other had gone on ahead with the dynamite while McTeague had assigned himself to the task of watching for interference. And McTeague had just declared with certainty that Melody had come alone. That meant that McTeague had been watching all along. Possibly McTeague had seen Melody climb the slope and had been keeping an eye on him since and had waited for this moment to show himself. But why? McTeague could have picked Melody off at any time, preferably on the slope. There was only one answer. McTeague had wanted to be sure that Melody had indeed come alone.

"You guessed wrong, McTeague," Melody said. "Since you boys were up to monkey business, we figured you'd play safe by leaving somebody behind. That notion made the slope mighty risky. So I told the boys to give me time to reach the rim before they started climbing — just to be on the safe side."

McTeague showed the whiteness of his teeth in what might have been a smile of derision, but, at the same time, he glanced over his shoulder. That made as much opportunity as Melody had hoped to gain, the only chance he would likely have. He didn't try for his gun. McTeague would be expecting that, and McTeague would be instinctively prepared for such a move. Instead, Melody flung himself sidewards, lunging toward his guitar propped nearby; and McTeague, sensing the movement, fired. The bullet chipped rock behind Melody and went ricocheting, but now Melody had grasped the guitar, and he flung it at McTeague.

There was no time for careful aiming. This whole play was born of desperation, and the guitar, arcing through the air, its silver plating catching the sunlight, didn't even graze McTeague. But, as the instrument came sailing, McTeague instinctively lurched sideways, and this movement cost him his balance. He fired as he fell, the bullet going wild, and he fell almost on top of Melody. But Melody was ready for him — ready enough to get his arms around McTeague; and the two, locked together and wedged down among the rocks, began a desperate exchange of blows.

Melody had been close enough to death to be possessed of a great anger, and when he got McTeague beneath him, Melody knew that the fight was won. A wiry strength was in McTeague, and Hardin's hired killer was desperate, too, but the man was nowhere near the adversary Breed Lenoir had been. Melody's real concern was that Hardin's other hand, who was doubtless somewhere in the vicinity, might be on the run now, fetched by those two shots. Wresting McTeague's ivory-handled gun from the man, Melody got to a stand and said hoarsely, "Get up, mister! Get up and hoist those hands!"

McTeague obeyed sullenly, and Melody removed McTeague's neckerchief and used it to tie the gunman's hands behind him. This done, Melody sought his guitar, thrusting McTeague's gun into the waistband of his own trousers as he went clambering over the rocks. The guitar seemed to have suffered no damage other than that the silver plating had been scarred; and Melody slung the instrument upon his back. "Now," he said as he returned to McTeague, "we'll have a look for your friend."

"You won't find him," McTeague retorted woodenly.

Melody was already wondering about that; he'd been certain the shots would fetch McTeague's partner, but the man had not put in an appearance. Was the fellow at this very moment skulking among the rocks, intending to size up the situation before showing himself? That seemed likely, so Melody, keeping carefully to cover, forced McTeague ahead as they ventured along the rim. A half-hour of this brought no results, and the going became increasingly rough.

"If your pard's lighted a fuse, it must be a long one," Melody remarked.

"He's got his orders," McTeague said. "The

dynamite doesn't go off till Weaver's cows are in the pass. Quirt wants the Cinnibar to remember this lesson. Yucca knows dynamite, and Yucca was told to keep out of sight and do his job, no matter what."

For McTeague this was a long speech, and even though it was delivered in a flat, toneless way, Melody sensed an edge of triumph in the gunman's voice. McTeague, captured, was wringing such delight as he could out of the fact that nothing had changed, really. McTeague and his partner had planned a pat hand — the one to loose the dynamite, the other to keep watch; and the charge was to be exploded regardless. But where? Looking for a man in this crazy country was a considerable chore.

Melody said grimly, "You've got a pretty good idea where your pard's hiding, mister. There might be a way of *making* you talk!"

"Torture?" McTeague's eyes showed contempt. "You won't do it. That's the trouble with your kind of man. You're hell-on-wheels in your own way, but you play by a set of rules, and they hamstring you every time. Torture ain't in your line."

Looking at this man, Melody felt a growing revulsion, but, at the same time, he was seeing the difference between McTeague and himself. Hardin's gun-hand was the type who considered the results — not the method by which they were attained. With the situation reversed, McTeague would be making a try at forcing the truth out of Melody; and it was this trait that made McTeague invaluable to his master. Yet McTeague had put his finger on a truth: Torture wasn't in Melody Malone's line. So, Melody could only say, "Come along. We'll keep looking!"

By noon they had moved many miles to the south along the rim, and always the country remained the same, broken and boulder-littered, gaunt clumps of bushes and occasional gnarled trees showing. Sometimes they were able to reach the rim and look down into the canyon; sometimes they were forced to circle a great distance to avoid clambering over mazes of rocks. Melody examined some of these rock clusters, forcing the silent, sweating McTeague along with him; but to no avail. A hawk wheeled silently overhead, the stillness of the hills remained unbroken; and Hardin's man, Yucca, was not to be seen.

With the sun standing high, Melody faced about in the opposite direction. He was now convinced that the dynamiter would hardly have penetrated this far south, but he wished he knew more about the handling of explosives, for such knowledge might have given him a clue as to where to expect Hardin's man.

There were a score of places where a charge, properly planted, would doubtless loosen enough rock to close the canyon. Somewhere along the rim, they had probably passed the lurking dynamiter.

They came all the way back to the slope, the return trip fruitless, yet it had not been possible to examine every foot of the rim. Melody was now acutely conscious of hunger, as well as a great weariness, and there was scant consolation to be gained from the fact that McTeague was obviously as worn as himself. Riding boots were not designed for walk. Food was below, in the saddle-bag Anita had provided, and Melody forced McTeague down the slope ahead of him and to the horse. Helping himself to a sandwich, Melody hesitated, then unbound McTeague's hands and handed the man food.

"Thanks," McTeague said dryly, but the contempt was in his eyes again — the contempt of a man who considered human kindness in another as a weakness.

It was therefore McTeague's own thirst, Melody judged, that prompted the man to afterwards indicate where a water jug could be found, beneath the seat of the Quirt wagon. The two having tilted this jug, Melody again forced McTeague ahead of him, and they went up the slope, Melody leaving the prisoner until that steep ascent was behind them. Lashing McTeague's hands with the neckerchief, Melody lifted his eyes to the south and saw, far out upon the vista stretching below them, a banner of dust. McTeague said, "Weaver, I reckon. You'll know where that dynamite is mighty soon." Melody said hoarsely, "Come on, damn you! There's still time to do some more looking!"

Weaver, if Melody was any judge of distance, had made very good time to-day; either that, or the Anvil had gotten off to an early start. Which meant that the showdown would come much sooner; once those cattle were edging into the pass, the explosion would let go, and Cinnibar Range would have a graphic example of what came of attempting to buck Quirt Hardin. All of which gave Melody the devil's own choice. Should he head south and warn the Anvil that the explosion was imminent? But Dallas Spade had doubtless warned Weaver of the possible danger. The dynamiter would still have to be flushed out of hiding, so Melody hurried McTeague ahead of him, making that endless, futile search of the rim.

Often the gunman stumbled and fell; McTeague was handicapped by having his hands lashed, but Melody began to sense that the man's constant tripping was calculated to slow the search, and he began hauling McTeague erect with scant ceremony. The afternoon wore on; they veered southward almost as far as they'd gone the first time. And then Melody stopped in his tracks.

He was so weary that his mind had gotten fuzzy. He'd grown tired of rocks and more rocks, of constant clambering and useless looking, and now he'd sensed a truth that might have come sooner if weariness hadn't blunted him. Yucca must be hiding near the slope. The dynamiter would have to know just when to light the fuse; this timing would have to be gauged to so many minutes, and that meant that the fellow would be posted where he could measure the progress of that oncoming trail herd. This in turn meant that he'd have to be stationed somewhere near the mouth of the canyon. And with this truth bursting upon him, Melody faced about.

But once again he was impressed with the futility of his own efforts. Even if his theory were correct, that still meant a considerable stretch of canyon rim to be minutely scoured. When the two of them came staggering to the maze of rocks where Melody had overcome McTeague, Melody was desperate enough to be reckless of consequences. To the south he could see the dust thickly swirling, and now he could hear the bawling of cattle, the popping of rope ends, as the herd was hazed onward. The Anvil had almost reached the pass.

Would Weaver and his crew pause now, reconnoitering before they advanced further? Or, finding the canyon open, would they presume that he, Melody, had prevented the explosion and thereby made it safe for them to forge onward? And now Melody was stricken by a new thought that left him aghast. Supposing Spade hadn't reached the Anvil in time this morning? Supposing Weaver had no awareness of possible danger? There was not now time to get down the slope and head off that herd. Frantic, Melody freed his gun and levelled it at McTeague. "You're going to call Yucca," Melody snapped. "You're going to call him every ten steps from here on."

"Reckon not," McTeague said.

"You're going to call him, or you're going to get a bullet in the brisket!"

McTeague showed the white of his teeth. "You wouldn't shoot a gent who has his hands tied behind him. It ain't in your line."

"You're wrong," Melody said calmly. "Sam Weaver will be riding point with that herd. When he comes into the canyon ahead of his cattle, he may be under the rock that will be blasted down. As I see it, it's his life or yours, McTeague. And him I call neighbour."

McTeague said, "To hell with you!"

Melody cocked the gun, and something was

born in McTeague's eyes that Melody had never seen there before. And here again was the difference between them; each man had his code, and that made for their strength and their weakness. Threatened by a gun, Melody might have defied the gun. But McTeague lifted his voice. *"Hey, Yucca?"* he called.

Silence . . . silence broken only by that growing sound of bawling cattle and popping rope ends and the clatter of many hooves over rocky ground. And then, from somewhere off yonder on the rim's edge, a voice raised cautiously: "That you, Mac?"

Melody peered frantically, trying to orient that sound. Yucca was no more than fifty yards from where Melody and his prisoner stood; of that Melody was sure. And he was also reasonably sure that he knew from which direction Yucca had spoken. He took a step in that direction, and McTeague lifted his voice again. *"Yucca! Light the fuse! Malone's on your trail!"*

There was in McTeague this peculiar code of courage, this lasting loyalty to his salt, and these had done their damage. Blind with fury, Melody swung upon the man, lifting his gun barrel and bringing it down across McTeague's skull. No time now to reflect that striking a helpless man wasn't in the Malone line; there was a greater need to remember. And as McTeague went to his knees, stunned,

Melody was running frantically, running in the direction from which Yucca had spoken.

Rocks barred the way. Melody clambered over them with no consideration for his hands and knees. The sweat was out on him; it seemed that the sounds of the Anvil's progress, magnified by the thin air, were growing louder, nearer. That herd wasn't stopping at the canyon's mouth!

But Melody was nearing the rim. He heard the scrape of bootsoles against rocky footing, the grunt of a man straining with effort. He clambered around a huge boulder and saw the head and shoulders of the man — one of those who'd ridden with Hardin the night the Quirt crew had almost hanged Melody. Apparently there was a ledge below the rim at this point, and a trail leading up from the ledge, for Yucca was just getting back to the rim. And that meant that behind the man the dynamite had been planted and the fuse lighted.

Yucca spied Melody at the same moment that the troubadour sighted Hardin's man. Yucca's torso and legs came into view; and Yucca was clawing a gun out of his holster. A great fear contorted the man's stubbled face — a fear all out of proportion to whatever danger Melody's presence presented; and Melody knew of what that fear was made. The dynamite below Yucca. And Melody, lifting his own gun, fired once, and, firing, knew he'd missed. But his bullet drove Yucca down out of sight below the rim.

"For gawd's sake, man, let me out of here!" Yucca called from wherever he clung. *"It's a three minute fuse I lighted!"*

"Jerk it out!" Melody advised. "Jerk the fuse before it goes off!"

"There ain't time!" Yucca shrieked, and he was speaking the truth. For whatever else he might have said was lost in the *Hrr—umpf!* of exploding dynamite.

There could be no telling now just how far below the rim that ledge had been where Yucca had planted the dynamite. The ground shaking, Melody tried wedging himself down into the litter of rocks as debris rained around him; and the taste of defeat was in his mouth. Rocks — tons of rocks — were roaring in a descent, and dust rose chokingly from them; and when Melody dared lift his head, the rim had moved a good many feet nearer to him, and that meant the ledge was gone, and the trail from it, and Yucca, too, was gone — destroyed in the blast of his own making.

Wearily Melody clambered back to where he'd left McTeague. The man was groaning back to consciousness, and Melody got him to his feet and shoved him toward the slope. Down below, he could hear the hoarse shouts of men and a great clamour, a thunder made insignificant by the thunder of the explosion which had inspired it. The Anvil cattle, stirred to a frenzy of fear by the blast had turned tail and were stampeding northward. And Melody, listening, judged that the Anvil hands were going after the herd.

Shaken by his experience, Melody got down the slope with McTeague ahead of him, and when the two came to where the Quirt wagon and horses were hidden, Melody unhobbled one of the animals, forced McTeague to its back, then fashioned a lead rope by hacking up the harness with a knife he found on McTeague. His prisoner readied for transportation, Melody got his own horse, tightened the cinch and stepped up into the saddle.

He didn't even pause to look into the Pass of the Blackrobes before he turned wearily northward. He knew what the explosion had done. Yucca had lighted the fuse sooner than he'd intended, and thus the blast had been set off before the Anvil herd had actually got into the canyon. The greater disaster had been averted, but Quirt Hardin had succeeded in spite of that. The back door to the Cinnibar was closed. . . . Closed for all time.

Chapter XVI
What Floren Found

Dusk had gathered when Melody reached the C-C Connected, fetching McTeague with him. They had met no one on their trip northward from the pass, though they had sighted a cow or two, bearing the Anvil brand. Weaver's crew was doubtless off yonder somewhere, scouring darkness, searching out the scattered, stampeded cattle. Melody and McTeague had ridden wearily, saying nothing to each other; and they found Chance Corday's ranch silent and deserted, no light showing in any of the buildings. The crew was out at the round-up camp, of course, unless Spade had taken the bulk of the men to join forces with the Anvil on to-day's disastrous drive. Probably C-C's foreman had persuaded Anita to stay at Weaver's place meanwhile. Spade wouldn't have cottoned to the idea of leaving Anita alone at the C-C. Not when Quirt Hardin had grown so bold as to start playing with dynamite.

The horses turned into a corral, Melody got a lamp burning in the cook-shack and prepared hot food for himself and his prisoner. Afterwards he escorted McTeague to a saddle shed, got a rope and did a more thorough job of binding the man. He left McTeague sprawled upon the hard planking of the floor. "I'll be turning you over to the sheriff," Melody promised. "Just as soon as I get on speaking terms with him."

No means was at hand whereby the saddle shed could be firmly locked, but Melody put his reliance in the rope now binding McTeague. Stepping back into the ranchyard, Melody gazed longingly at the bunkhouse and would have liked nothing better than a few hours' sleep. But he put his mind against this need and climbed the slight rise of ground to where Chance Corday's grave was located. It took only a moment's examination to convince him that the dirt had been freshly turned. Otis Floren had obeyed his injunction to fetch a doctor out here to-day for an examination of Corday's remains.

With a sigh, Melody again gazed at the bunkhouse, but went resolutely to the corral instead. Dropping a rope on his own horse, the mount he'd swapped for a C-C saddler last night, he got gear on to the horse, and, within a few minutes, he was heading northward toward Stanton

City. Otis Floren was going to have news that might very well prove to be interesting; and there was only one way to get that news.

He paralleled the wagon road but kept at a distance from it, and by this means Melody came in due time to The Strip, reaching the fence a bit west of the gate. As he'd done the night before, he lifted his horse over the wire and made the jump again on the far side, envying the cayuse its resiliency and wishing that he, himself, felt half as frisky. His sleepless hours were beginning to tell on him. And, since the range seemed deserted, he resorted to an old expedient for keeping himself awake. The guitar removed from his back, he cuddled it close and turned his mind to the saga of the girl on Chowder Creek, her money-minded suitor and his gargantuan rival:

> "I'm diggin' me a bear trap on Chowder Creek,
> Aim to ketch a grizzly that walks on two feet,
> Hi, yo, diddle, di, day. . . .
> And when my rival comes a-courtin' Maisie,
> He's in for a fall that'll shake him up crazy,
> 'Cause that trap's in the trail, and she's sure a daisy,
> Hi, yo, diddle, di, da-a-a-y. . . ."

Which, Melody reflected, showed you how inefficient a fellow got when he was missing his sleep. Creek and feet didn't rhyme worth a whoop and a holler; but he slung the guitar upon his back again and decided that revision could wait until another day. After that he fell to dozing in the saddle. His horse must have had fond recollections of the oat bin in the Stanton City livery stable, for the mount headed onward unerringly, and Melody awoke with a start to find himself sitting his saddle before that fragrant establishment.

Considerably refreshed from the doze he'd had, Melody dismounted, and his first glance was toward the jail building; and he was relieved to find Anse Crain's office darkened. Except for the roistering element whose horses thronged the hitch-rails of the many saloons, Stanton City was bedded down for the night. No light showed in Floren's quarters over the mercantile store, but Melody, after waiting for a pair of wayfarers to get on down the boardwalk, again shinnied up a porch support and clambered to the sloping roof and drummed his knuckles on the partially-raised window of Floren's bedroom. There was that same rustling of blankets and padding of bare feet upon a floor. The sash squeaked as it was raised, and Floren, wearing his nightcap, peered forth.

"Oh, it's you!" Floren said with considerable relief.

"Who were you expecting?" Melody inquired. "What a way to do business! A bald-complected professor fellow once told me a story about a pair of people who used to get together in this fashion quite regular. Romeo and Juliet, he called 'em."

The levity went out his voice. "Where's Anse Crain?" he asked.

"Gone looking for you," Floren said. "After you'd left last night, I went over to his office and let him out of his bracelets and brought him around. He didn't even wait to ask questions. I'd say that he's smelling out your trail like a hound dog tracking a 'coon."

"Open the window a mite higher and I'll come inside," Melody said. Floren obeyed, and Melody eased into the room, groped in the darkness and seated himself upon the edge of Floren's rumpled bed.

"My story's short — but it's not very sweet," Melody said. "I headed for the pass last night and stopped off at the C-C first to have Dallas Spade tell Sam Weaver what the Anvil might expect. McTeague was up on the rim above the canyon, and another Quirt hand, a fellow called Yucca, had come with him. I got McTeague's twine tangled, but he wouldn't tell me where his partner was planting the dynamite. I located that dynamite just three minutes before it went off. The pass is closed, Floren."

The lawyer drew in a long breath. "The Anvil — ?" he ventured.

"Safe enough, I reckon. They were so close to the canyon that the explosion stampeded the herd. I haven't had a chance to find out what's happened since. I fetched McTeague back to the C-C and penned him up in the saddle shed. If you happen to see Anse Crain, you can tell him I've got a customer for his calaboose any time he wants to take delivery."

Floren shook his head. "I wonder if that's going to get us any place? Hardin will just repudiate McTeague and swear that what the Quirt hands were doing in the hills wasn't by his orders. And McTeague will probably keep silent and bear out Hardin — knowing that Hardin in the long run, will find a way to get him out of jail."

"McTeague's loyal enough to his salt," Melody agreed. "But you tell Anse Crain about him, just the same. How did you and Doc What's-his-name make out to-day? I had a look at Chance Corday's grave. It had been opened. That's really what fetched me to town."

"I took Doc Bishop to the C-C, just as you suggested," Floren said. "We got there in mid-morning and found nobody around. Anita

Corday had left a note in the ranch-house for you, a note saying she was going to the Anvil with Dallas Spade and would stay with Mrs. Weaver for the time being. I'd have liked to have gotten her permission before touching the grave."

"I told you last night not to worry about legal procedure. What did you find?"

"Doc Bishop made the examination. I haven't the stomach for that kind of work. I don't know upon what you based your guesswork, Malone, but you certainly guessed right. I've a written report which Doc Bishop made for me. Chance Corday's skull wasn't crushed, as you suspected, but one thing is absolutely certain, even though Doc Bishop's examination was necessarily brief and not made under the best of conditions. A bullet was put into Chance. Not through the heart, as you guessed, but through the head. You were right about Chance Corday being murdered."

Melody whistled softly. "They fixed him for sure," he mused. "Then they set the fire so that what was left of Corday wouldn't be inspected too closely. And where was Mr. Quirt Hardin that night?"

Floren's white nightgown sleeves moved in the darkness as he spread his hands in a gesture. "Anse Crain wondered about that at the time. Crain didn't suspect there was a bullet in Chance, and he figured that the fire was probably an accident — but there was, of course, the possibility that it had been set. Crain once told me that he'd checked up and was satisfied that Hardin and his crew were at the Quirt at the time the fire broke out at the C-C."

Melody smiled. "We'll see," he said.

"I'm glad you showed up here to-night," Floren said. "For another reason. When I got back from the ranch this afternoon, a cattle-buyer was waiting to see me. He'd just gotten into town, and he'd been told that I was a sort of business agent for some of the ranchers. The fellow is still here; he put up at the Belle Fourche. He wants cattle in a hurry, and he's willing to pay spot cash and a bonus for delivery to Stanton City, and he'll handle the shipping himself. Stock cars will be shunted here to-morrow. It's a good offer, and I sent one of the town loafers to carry the word to Dallas Spade."

Melody nodded, and Floren said, "It looks like the C-C has the best chance to cash in on that offer. Hennessey can't very well sell the Lazy-L herd — not until Rocky Lynch's brother gets here, anyway. You said the Anvil herd was scattered by the explosion. That means Sam Weaver will have to spend a couple of days rounding up the stuff. The C-C is the one outfit ready to move beef. But you're still the legal head of the outfit. It's up to you to decide whether the ranch tries to fill that order."

Melody said, "You can climb into your pants and go find yourself a horse, old-timer. I've got to do my bossing of the C-C from a long distance away, since Anse Crain is cutting sign on me. But I want you to get word to Dallas Spade that it's my order that we're trying for that bonus. You'll likely find Spade either at Weaver's place, or at the C-C round-up camp. Our gather should be just about finished."

"But what about The Strip?" Floren asked. "With that bonus, you could afford to pay Hardin's toll and still come out ahead of the game. Is that your idea?"

Melody frowned. "I'd forgotten about The Strip for the moment. No, we won't be paying Quirt Hardin his toll. In fact, I've a hunch he wouldn't let us cross at any price. News of the cattle-buyer's offer is going to get around fast. Chances are, Hardin knows of it already. And that's where Hardin's got the Injun sign on everybody. He can keep The Strip closed, round up his own stuff, and collect that bonus."

"Then there's no use of my carrying word to Dallas Spade, Malone. He couldn't move the C-C gather any farther than the south fence of The Strip."

Melody shaped up a cigarette and got it going and drew long and thoughtfully at the tobacco. At last he said, "You get word to Spade just the same. This is the showdown for sure, Floren. Rocky Lynch had his try at the fence, and he went at it in his own bullheaded way and died trying. Sam Weaver chose to turn his back on the fence, and that failed, too; the pass is closed — and Quirt Hardin closed it. Now it's C-C's turn to try crashing across The Strip, and, the way things have shaped up, we'll have to try alone. Yes, you tell Spade to bunch the cattle and head them north. I don't think he'll find anybody guarding the gate when he gets there. I'll see to that."

Floren's hand moved in the darkness, and his fingers closed on Melody's arm. "I put my chips on you, boy," Floren said huskily. "I sized you up that first day and gambled that you were the one that Chance Corday had had in his mind. But I was just a man dreaming out loud. Later, everybody thought I was wrong in my guess — and sometimes I began to wonder myself. Then you decided to fight. I don't know what you've got in your head now, but I don't think I want you to try it. That fence isn't as important as your life. Not to me, anyway."

Melody said, "There's been too much talking and thinking about that damn' fence. There's been too much scheming as to how to get around three strands of barbed wire. In worrying about Hardin's fence, everybody lost sight of the real barrier. It's Hardin himself who's got to be toppled over, not his fence. When Hardin falls, his fence falls too. And until Hardin digs his fat nose into the dust, this range isn't going to be worth living on. That's the way I've come to see it. And that's what I'll be keeping in my mind when I ride out of here to-night. I won't tell you what I'm up to. I'm not sure myself, how I'm going to work it. But tell Spade to start moving those cattle. The C-C is making its try. I'll see to it that nobody blocks the way."

Chapter XVII
In Killer's Clothing

And so, once again, Melody Malone came across the moonlit miles out of Stanton City, heading southward toward the C-C Connected. Behind him this night, Otis Floren would also be riding, carrying word to Dallas Spade in accordance with Melody's instructions. Melody might have waited for the lawyer, but strong in Melody was a consciousness that whatever he was to do must be done quickly, and that made the minutes precious. With the first streak of dawn the C-C herd would be pointed north, and Melody had pledged that The Strip would be unguarded. Just how he was to bring that miracle about, he didn't know. But there was the germ of an idea in Melody, and from such a beginning he was perfecting his plan.

The whole situation was very simple when reduced to its rudiments. You gave the Curling Quirt something to do that was more important than guarding The Strip. With this accomplished, the C-C could pass through the gates unchallenged. Unfortunately, the planning of such a coup required some cogitating. Melody was reminded of the prospector who declared that if he only had some ham, he would have ham and eggs for breakfast, provided he could get some eggs.

But there was that germ of an idea, and Melody was smiling grimly when he reached The Strip. He jumped the fence without mishap, though not with as many inches to spare as on previous occasions. His horse was feeling the miles it had covered to-night, but it got over the second fence, too. The range lay ethereal in the moonlight, misty and still and empty. Three times in the last two nights Melody had crossed The Strip without getting so much as a glimpse of Hardin's crew, and, for a space, he wondered if Quirt Hardin's men had taken to occupying themselves elsewhere and had ceased patrolling the wire.

But that didn't make sense. If Hardin had heard of the cattle-buyer who was offering quick cash for delivery to Stanton City, Hardin might have put his crew to gathering the Quirt herd. At the same time, though, Hardin would be even more mindful of the need to keep an eye on his wire, thus making sure that no south range rancher was hurrying cattle to town. No, Hardin would be more alert than ever. There were many miles of wire, and it had just been Melody's luck to have crossed at points where none of the Quirt crew happened to be watching at the moment. The peacefulness of this night was a delusion. Off yonder, and probably not far away, gun-hung riders were on the watch.

And Sheriff Anse Crain was out here somewhere, too, doggedly looking for a certain elusive fugitive given to guitar playing and the creation of verses of doubtful merit. And this, Melody reflected, would be a mighty poor time to run into that redoubtable pillar of the law. There'd be no persuading Crain that Melody had important work to do. Not by a jugful. It would be the Stanton City calaboose — and no back talk about it.

Thus Melody rode with an eye to making the minutes count, but he rode with a certain wariness, too, and with the thought that he'd definitely grown unpopular with an awful lot of people. But he was to see neither friend nor foe on that ride; and when he came again to the C-C Connected, well after midnight, he found that same dark and deserted air that had characterised the ranch when he had fetched McTeague up from the Pass of the Blackrobes, a prisoner.

McTeague was still cooling his heels. This

Melody learned after quickly turning his horse into a corral and going to the saddle shed for a look. Finding a lantern, Melody got it to burning and suspended it from a peg. Then he stooped and began untying McTeague, the gunman watching him in that inscrutable silence that was McTeague's constant cloak. When Hardin's man was free, Melody gave him a minute to chafe his wrists and restore circulation; and then Melody said, "Undress, mister."

"Undress — ?"

"Peel right down to whatever you use for underwear at this season. And do it pronto."

Stubbornness gave McTeague's face a grimmer cast, but Melody tapped his gun. "Haven't you learned yet that I'm through fooling around with you?" Melody demanded. "Get those clothes off before I clout you over the head and peel you myself."

With a shrug of surrender, McTeague began divesting himself of his black garments; and Melody removed his own clothes, keeping at a distance from McTeague and making sure that at no time was he so encumbered as to be unable to reach his gun quickly. But McTeague made no aggressive move. When both men stood in their undergarments, Melody said, "I'm going to tie you up again. You can put on my clothes first, if you want. Might be kind of cold before sunrise."

Shrugging again, McTeague reached for Melody's discarded Levis and faded shirt, and Melody, at the same time, began pulling on the gunman's garb. Both were about of a size, tall and lean, and each got a reasonable fit out of the swap. Melody had a little trouble with a string tie McTeague had worn, but at last he knotted it to his satisfaction. The killer's black clothing completely donned, Melody went to work with the rope again, tying McTeague. This done, Melody snuffed out the lantern, left the shed, and closed the door behind him.

His plan had reached this stage of perfection: he was going to Curling Quirt's headquarters, and he was going as McTeague, knowing such an impersonation could not stand the test of careful scrutiny, but gambling that the deception would serve him to some degree. Neither McTeague nor himself had shaved for at least two nights and a day, and their stubble heightened the resemblance. And if there was time enough to take advantage of what darkness was left, there was a gambler's chance that the ruse might get a man safely inside the Quirt stronghold.

What would happen then was something Melody preferred to let shape itself when the time came. McTeague's ivory-handled gun in

McTeague's holster, and his own gun left inside the bunkhouse, along with his guitar, Melody went to the corral and got the Quirt horse that had helped haul a dynamite-laden wagon to the Pass of the Blackrobes and had then served to tote McTeague to the C-C. Melody might have loaded a saddle upon this horse and taken a bridle from the C-C's plentitude of such gear; but he didn't. He wanted to look as McTeague might have looked had the gunman come directly from the pass, so he fashioned a hackamore out of rope, then mounted to the bare back of the horse and headed along the wagon road that led northward.

There wasn't much speed in the mount. A work horse, the animal was docile enough to permit the indignity of a man upon its back, but it was used to plodding along ahead of a wagon, and no dint of effort had any real effect on increasing its pace. But Melody at last managed to get it to a gallop, and in this manner he came up the road to the gate in the south fence of The Strip — the gate he had so studiously avoided these last two nights. The moon was settling to the west now; the light was dim and uncertain, but there was enough to show Melody the man who reared upward, a rifle in his hands, on the far side of the gate. Here was the first test, but this guard, peering intently, cried: "Mac! Where the devil you been? The boss expected you back hours ago."

Melody tugged McTeague's sombrero a half-inch lower and made a flat, impatient gesture with his hand. The guard quickly unfastened the gate and hauled it aside, and, as Melody prodded the horse through the passage, the guard said, "Where's Yucca?"

"Dead," Melody muttered, and, having managed to confine his end of the conversation to this single word, he kicked a show of speed out of the horse and put the guard behind him.

That had been a bad moment there at the gate, but at least he'd learned that his impersonation was adequate. McTeague, he'd been told, was a man given to economising his speech, and he blessed the gunman for this trait. And then, The Strip almost crossed, he steeled himself for another ordeal. Not far ahead would be the other gate and a second sentry.

This man proved to be a twin to the first in quick and ready wariness, and he, too, said, "Mac!" when Melody came to a stop. Again Melody made that flat, impatient gesture with his hand; the guard leaned his rifle against the wire and fumbled at the fastening of the gate and swung it wide, but, just as Melody prodded his horse into the opening, this second sentry cried: *"You're not McTeague!"*

He was lunging toward the rifle as he shouted, but the movement brought him a step nearer Melody. And Melody acted instinctively. He got McTeague's ivory-handled gun out of leather, and he brought the barrel down across the guard's skull. The fellow groaned, his knees unhinging, and as he collapsed, Melody spilled off his horse and bent over him. This had been no part of Melody's plan, this having to render a guard *hors de combat,* and he wished now that he'd avoided the gate and tried jumping the fence instead. But the work horse he was using for a mount hadn't seemed capable of such an effort, and that had left Melody with no choice. And now he had an unconscious sentry on his hands.

Using the man's neckerchief, he tied the fellow's hands behind his back. The guard's gun-belt he used to lash the man's ankles. Then Melody hauled the unconscious form along the wire for a good fifty yards, and left the fellow. A handkerchief in McTeague's coat pocket made a fairly effective gag; and this was the best Melody could do. But a new concern was beginning to ride him. Were these sentries changed at hourly intervals? Or were other Quirt hands, patrolling the wire, likely to stumble upon this man? If that happened, the fat would be in the fire. Yet the night was almost over, and there wasn't time to haul the guard to a place of concealment.

No, he'd have to take his chance that his own exposure wouldn't come of this, and, so thinking, Melody returned to the ancient horse, closed the gate, crawled to the mount's back and turned east. From here on the going was guesswork. He'd never visited the Curling Quirt, and his idea of the location of the ranch-buildings was hazy, dependent upon what little he'd overheard on the subject while he'd worked with the C-C round-up crew. But he kept in the general direction which reason told him was right, and at the first flush of dawn he looked upon the pretentious buildings which were Hardin's headquarters.

There were horses in the corrals, he noticed, and a few men moving from the long bunk-house to the big red barn; but no smoke lifted from the ranch-house itself. Melody brought the horse to a stop before the long, low gallery fronting the place. He'd been spied by those men out in the yard; McTeague's name was called, but Melody paid no heed. Climbing briskly to the gallery, he entered the house as boldly as though he'd been here a hundred times. And then, closing the door behind him, he paused, listening.

So far, so good. He was presuming that

Hardin bedded down here, rather than in the bunkhouse with his crew; and he was presuming, too, that Hardin was in the house. If these presumptions were right, such Quirt hands as had seen his arrival would suppose that he'd gone inside to report to Hardin. Thus he was comparatively safe for the moment, though he had the feeling of a man walking upon thin ice. He looked about a living-room littered with costly furniture which bulked dimly in the grey and uncertain light, and then he grinned as the sound of lusty snoring reached him from a room adjacent to the one in which he found himself.

Yonder was Quirt Hardin's bedroom, and when Melody stepped silently into it, he saw the bulk of Hardin beneath a tangle of blankets. Stepping to the man's side, Melody shook him roughly, shook him again, and saw Hardin's little eyes open. Hardin appraised him sleepily and said, "Where the devil have you been keeping yourself?" Then the man was suddenly wide awake and sitting up in bed. "*You!*" he ejaculated, but McTeague's ivory-handled gun was lined on him.

"Get up!" Melody ordered grimly. "Get up and pile into your clothes. And move lively. No funny motions, now! I'd just as soon kill you as shoot a rattlesnake. And you make a heap bigger target!"

The hate he'd seen in Hardin's eyes the day they'd first met was there again, but Hardin kicked back the blankets and put his bare feet to the floor and came to a stand, a huge, ungainly creature in the long red underwear which was his sleeping garb. He began dressing, moving altogether too slowly for Melody's liking, and several times Melody gestured with the gun to hurry Hardin. When the fat man was finally dressed, he glared at Melody. "Just what in blazes do you think you're doing?" Hardin demanded.

"You and me," Melody declared, "are going for a little ride. When we don't hurry back, your crew is going to come looking for us. That's as much as you need to know."

Hardin's eyes narrowed. "I can guess the rest. Your C-C bunch is anxious to move beef to town, eh? Yes, I've heard about the cattle-buyer and his bonus. And you think that nobody will be watching The Strip if my crew's out hunting me."

"That," said Melody, "is the general idea. Only there's more to it. The rest I'm saving for a surprise. Do you like surprises, Hardin?"

Stepping sideways toward the one window in the room, Melody shot its shade upward and hoisted the sash a few inches. This window was set in the rear of the house, and from it Melody could see the barn and corrals, and the men moving about. "Just step over here," Melody ordered Hardin. "You're going to holler to your boys. You're going to say, 'Me and McTeague are taking a pasear. Saddle up two horses and bring them around to the gallery, boys.' You're going to say that — and not a word more. And you're going to say it so they'll understand that you mean business!"

Hardin hesitated, and the game might have been won or lost in this moment. But the gun was still in Melody's hand, and grim intensity made a mask of Melody's face, and Hardin must have read what could have been his death there. The man proved himself to be no fool. Waddling toward the window, he cupped his hands to his mouth and shouted his message word for word, just as Melody had directed.

Melody let a few minutes elapse and then said, "Now we'll be heading to the gallery." He lifted Hardin's gun and belt from the post of a chair and quickly jacked the shells out of the forty-five with the pearl-inlaid handle. "Put this on," he ordered. "You might look naked to the boys without it. But don't forget that the fangs have just been pulled."

Hardin sullenly donned the belt, and, with Melody at his elbow, the two came through the parlour and out upon the gallery. Melody had dumped McTeague's gun back into the holster, but his fingers were never far from it. A Quirt hand was just rounding the house, leading two saddled horses behind him. Melody began shaping up a cigarette, keeping his eyes on the paper between his fingers, and thus it was natural that his head was tilted downward and his sombrero brim shielded his face. He said, too softly for the Quirt hand to hear, "Send him about his business."

Hardin wasn't quick to obey, and Melody let paper and tobacco go fluttering and hooked a hand in his gun belt, not far from his holster. Hardin said, "O.K., Charley. That's all. Don't know just when I'll be back."

Charley left the two saddlers with reins trailing and vanished around a corner of the house; and Melody moved forward, nudging Hardin at the same time. The two came down from the gallery and lifted themselves into saddles, and Melody leaned and got his reins and Hardin's as well. They headed for the trail that climbed the slope that looked down upon the Quirt buildings, and this was the most breathless moment for Melody. Bluff and luck had brought him through to this point; another minute or two and he'd have Hardin out of the sight and the hearing of the crew. Hardin knew it too; a desperate fury was building in the man's balloon-like face; but there was nothing Hardin could do. And then, suddenly, a rider was skylined atop the slope, and this rider came roaring downward, galloping at a hard tilt toward Melody and his prisoner.

There was too much of desperate intent in the mien of that oncoming rider to indicate an ordinary arrival, and Melody's first jarring thought was that here was one of the sentries. That unconscious guard had been discovered, and this man was coming to warn the Quirt that something was amiss! But Melody knew differently when he had a better look. He recognised the Levis garbing the rider, and he recognised the battered sombrero; for it was his. And the man was McTeague.

No guessing how McTeague had freed himself from the C-C saddle shed. Getting out of the shed itself would have been comparatively easy; a stout shoulder thrown against the door would have turned the trick. The question was how McTeague had skinned out of the rope. And there was only one answer. Melody had tied McTeague tightly the first time, doing such a good job that Melody had been able to ride to Stanton City and back without McTeague freeing himself. But Melody had been in a tremendous hurry when he'd tied McTeague again, after swapping clothes with the man. And Melody, obviously, had not made the knots as secure.

McTeague had helped himself to a C-C saddler and gear, and McTeague had got a gun, too — possibly Melody's own which the troubadour had left in the bunkhouse. The gun was in McTeague's hand, and the man snapped a shot as he came roaring downward. Melody felt the air-lash of that bullet as he swerved sideways in his saddle, and, swerving, he clawed for the gun he carried. The gun in his hand, he had little consciousness of aiming, yet he knew his life hung on his skill at the moment. The gun bucked back against his palm; his horse and Hardin's reared frantically; but McTeague was flinging up his arms and spilling from the horse. He lighted rolling and sprawled to a grotesque stop, and something about the shapeless look of him told Melody the man was dead.

The poet in Melody saw the ironic justice in this, for McTeague had died as he had lived — died by his own ivory-handled gun, the weapon that was his trade mark and his creed. But this wasn't the time for reflections upon the workings of destiny. Not with the Quirt thoroughly aroused by that exchange of shots and men coming on the run, shouting questions as they charged around the house. The hornet's nest had been kicked over for sure.

Chapter XVIII
At Rope's End

Part of Melody's plan had included eventual exposure. His impersonation of McTeague was only to have served him in the bold stroke of getting into the ranch-house and out again with Hardin; after that he'd have taken steps in due time to let the Quirt know that its boss was in enemy hands. Thus Melody proposed to toll Hardin's crew away from The Strip to-day. But he hadn't intended being exposed so soon — or in such a fashion. He'd wanted a margin of safety first, but that margin had been denied him by circumstance. The crew, rushing now to the scene of the shooting, was going to realise quickly that since the dead man was McTeague, the man in McTeague's clothing was an impostor.

No, this was not at all as Melody had planned. His little masquerade was due to come to an abrupt end, and so, the gun still in his hand, he fired toward the oncoming men, his bullets sending some scurrying back around the corner of the house. At the same time, Melody kept a firm hold on the reins of Hardin's horse; and that was his saving. A few Quirt hands, quicker of wit and perception than the others, began shooting, but the closeness of Quirt Hardin to his captor was Melody's protection. Hardin, realising that Melody's danger was apt to be his own, was raising his voice in a frantic order to his men to hold their fire. And, with the crew hesitating, Melody prodded his mount, and, leading Hardin's horse, galloped up the slope and over the brow of it and out of the immediate danger of flying lead.

But he didn't tarry here. Behind him the ranch would be aboil with activity; men would be getting gear on to saddlers in record time and lining out in pursuit. His scant advantage would have to be utilised for all it was worth, so Melody took to the cover of a brushy coulee. McTeague had used this same coulee the day the gunman had manoeuvred to waylay Jake, but, instead of running the coulee's length as McTeague had done, Melody bored deep into the brush, dragging Hardin's horse behind him. Sheltered, Melody came to a stop and ground McTeague's gun into Hardin's side.

"They'll be coming pronto," Melody said

breathlessly. "I'm gambling that at first they'll be too excited to bother with tracking. One peep out of you at the wrong time and you're a gone gosling!"

Soon they could hear the thunder of hooves; Melody, listening intently, judged that at least half a dozen riders had topped the rise and gone roaring across the rangeland. When the sound had diminished, Melody unfastened a lariat which hung at his saddle-horn and bound Hardin's hands. Then he led his captive up out of the coulee. To the west a dust cloud lingered in the still morning air, indicating the direction of the Quirt's search. Melody promptly headed east.

He had to do much manoeuvring in the next couple of hours. He kept to whatever cover he could find, moving at first in a general easterly direction and then swinging north. Finally they headed toward the west. Hardin came along in a sullen silence, and, as they kept veering across the tawny rangeland, Melody from time to time managed to glimpse a faint and distant dust cloud which told him the pursuit was still in the saddle. Once, from a promontory, he was even able to do a haphazard job of counting heads, and he judged that nearly a dozen men were now in the search. Obviously the crew had been augmented by others who'd been patrolling the wire and had returned to the ranch at dawn to be told by the cook, perhaps, that a new need was to keep them in saddles. And, seeing how the pursuit had swelled, Melody grinned. Each man on his trail meant one less guarding The Strip. He had pledged that Dallas Spade would find no real obstacle at the fence. If luck held, Melody would keep that pledge.

And so, through the long morning, he kept heading westward, trailing the sullen Quirt owner behind him, and when the sun stood high they had almost reached the far wall of the Cinnibar, the mighty hills rearing above them. Now the land was more broken; endless waves of low hills seemed always to spread before them, and there was screening timber; but still the pursuit was on their trail. And those Quirt hands were clinging doggedly. Obviously they had long since ceased their aimless tactics of charging blindly across the rangeland in the hope of glimpsing Melody and their boss. They'd taken to tracking, a slower method but one more apt to bring them results. Thus, in a sense, Melody's danger was greater now than it had been a few hours before when he'd hidden in the coulee within shouting distance of the Quirt ranch-house. But the taste of triumph was in his mouth, for The Strip had been forsaken to-day.

Hunger and thirst had become a torture,

but his greatest need was for sleep, and this need was telling on him. Other than the dozing he'd done in the saddle on his way to Stanton City last night, he'd had no real sleep for two days and two nights. Quite often he found himself nodding now. Quirt Hardin, who'd been aroused from a comfortable bed just a few hours before, was under no such handicap. And though Hardin had apparently resigned himself to whatever fate had in store, Melody was not assured by the man's passivity. Hardin would seize any opportunity that presented itself, and Melody's weariness might give Hardin his chance. No man could go on for ever.

Realising this, Melody planned his next move. Dismounting and ordering Hardin to do likewise, Melody kept hold of the rope that fastened Hardin's wrists. Coiling the lariat over his left arm, Melody slapped the horses across their rumps, sending them galloping off to the east, in the direction of the distant Quirt. "We walk now," Melody said and began leading Hardin deeper into the hills. Soon they were stumbling along in what seemed to be aimless fashion, Hardin cursing low and monotonously, but Melody was gauging every footfall and picking rocky ground where their passage would leave little trace. Deeper into the timber, Melody came upon a creek, and, wading out into the icy water, he forced Hardin to follow as they strode along the creek for several hundred feet. Then they climbed to the far bank and struck off into timber again.

Soon Melody was more asleep than awake, but at last he found what he'd been seeking, an open space that was ringed by bushes and had a gnarled old tree in its centre. Wordlessly he forced Hardin to a sitting position at the base of the tree, and here he lashed the man. Hardin's fury unleashed itself then, and he tied a litany of vileness to Melody's name.

"You think you've won!" Hardin ranted. "You gambled that my crew wouldn't have brains enough to see through your real intention; and you were right. The damn fools are sticking to the trail instead of getting back to The Strip where they belong. But this is going to cost you your hide. One of those boys is a born tracker, and that gent will keep on your trail forever!"

Unknotting the neckerchief from about Hardin's thick throat, Melody said wearily, "I'd like to listen to you all day, but I've got other plans. So you get gagged, mister. Before many more hours, those boys of yours may be within hearing distance."

The gag cutting off Hardin's vehement outpouring, Melody, went a few paces away, stretched himself upon the ground, put McTeague's sombrero under his head for a pillow, and, within a minute, was fast asleep. If his ruse of turning the horses loose and covering the sign of his movements afoot afterwards was successful, he was comparatively safe. Yet if the Quirt crew, finding those riderless horses, persisted in combing these hills, sheer luck might bring them to this very spot. That was the chance Melody was taking. He had reached rope's end, and there was no going further.

For the next few hours he might have been dead for all the consciousness he had of his surroundings. His outraged body was demanding its dues, and he soaked up sleep as a sponge soaks up water. What finally awoke him was some sound so slight as to be beyond naming, some instinct that seeped down into a part of him that had managed to remain alert. And it brought him bolt upright. Night had come, he discovered; the moon had just risen, its light filtering through a canopy of leaves and needles to dapple this little clearing. Melody's eyes went to the tree where he'd left Hardin tied, and Hardin was still there. But Hardin, in the intervening hours, had been working at the rope. Hardin's hands were free, and the man plucked at the knots binding his ankles. Melody reached him in a bound, but he began struggling with the knots himself, to the Quirt owner's vast amazement.

"Get up," Melody ordered when he'd freed the man. "Take a walk around and start your circulation going." Hardin obeyed, Melody keeping a wary eye on him the while. Then Melody fished for the jack-knife that had been McTeague's, and with this he cut a short length from the end of the lariat, and used the bit of rope to bind Hardin's hands behind the fellow's back. Hardin began cursing again. "Another five minutes and I'd have been free and at your throat!" Hardin snapped. "My boys are in these woods, mister. About an hour ago, before I'd gotten that damned gag out of my mouth, I heard them threshing around."

Melody listened. The woods were silent save for the normal sounds of the night. An owl went gliding by with a faint flutter of wings; off in the distance the creek made gurgling music. Leaving Hardin standing, Melody did a bit of exploring. Near the clearing he found himself on the lip of a cut bank and from here a fairly open panorama spread below him. Off in the distance, to the east and a little to the north, the lights of Stanton City winked. The stars indicated that the night was not very far gone, and Melody sighed, wishing he could know what had transpired on the Cinnibar to-day. But the die was cast. In all likelihood the C-C herd was now in town and delivered.

Coming back to where he'd left Hardin, Melody grinned. Sleep had given Melody new vitality, and his usual good humour had been restored. Yet there was still a certain grim intensity about him that must have showed in his eyes; for Hardin said querulously, "What now — ?"

"If your boys passed by an hour ago, they should be an hour farther away by now," Melody said. "I'm gambling that we won't be disturbed for a spell. When I took you out of your bed this morning, I told you I had a surprise I was saving for you. Here it comes, Hardin. I'm going to tell you a story. If I had my guitar along, I'd put it to music. But you'll just have to take it as it is."

Hardin said, "What do I care about your blasted story!"

"Why, shucks," Melody said mildly, "it's about you — a fat hunk of poison who thought up a scheme to strangle your neighbours by fencing off a strip of ground. But there was one neighbour you were mighty scared of — a gent called Chance Corday. You reckoned you'd feel easier in your bones if Chance Corday was out of the way when you pulled your scheme, so you started figuring a way to get rid of him. It had to be a special way. Too many people — Sheriff Crain among 'em — were likely to think of you right quick if Corday was found dry-gulched."

Hardin ran his tongue along his lips and said, "Everybody knows Chance Corday died accidentally."

"Everybody? Jake, now, had a different idea, I'm thinking. Because Jake remembered just before the fire out at the C-C, you came to town and adopted that big tom-cat, Brutus. You said you wanted him for a mouser, but later on you bought fish for the cat. A kind-hearted act for a gent who's proved he packs a stone inside his chest where his ticker ought to be. Some people wouldn't have made any tie-up in their minds between a cat, a fish, and a fire — but Jake did. Jake was the sort of fellow to have known of every crooked scheme that was ever worked, because Jake was nine-tenths crook himself. It happened that I'd heard of that particular scheme, too. That's one thing that comes from travelling — you get broadened. The scheme was one that's been worked a dozen times in a dozen places, likely — usually by gents who insure their property and then set it afire to collect the insurance. There's a good many ways a fire can be set, but the cat and the scheme is one of the most fool-proof."

Hardin's ponderous face had taken on the

colour of wet putty. "Meaning — ?" he demanded.

"Meaning that you and some of your boys took a pasear over to the C-C one night. Chance Corday was alone; his crew was on round-up. One of you put a bullet through Corday's head. Doc Bishop examined the body yesterday, and he can verify that. You had Chance dead, but that wasn't so good. If he was found shot in his own ranch-house, Anse Crain might pay *you* a visit. But a fire would destroy the signs. The fire might also have fetched in the round-up crew from the range. You didn't want to be found close to the C-C with the ranch-house ablaze, but you'd thought all that out in advance. So you'd fetched Brutus and his fish along. All you had to do then was to loop a bit of twine around the base of a kerosene lamp and tie a fish to the end of that twine, leaving the fish dangling above the floor. That's usually the way the stunt is worked. You gave Brutus a smell of the fish, and then you probably put him outside, but you left a window open for him. Then you rode off."

"You're crazy!" Hardin exploded.

"Brutus likely has a long memory for the smell of fish. So Brutus hung around the C-C, looking for a way to get in. After a while he found that open window; you had to gamble on how long that would take him. But at last he made it, and when he clawed at the fish, he just naturally pulled the lamp off the table, or wherever you'd perched it, and started a fire. But he'd given you time to be a long way from the C-C — so far away that Anse Crain was later satisfied that you couldn't have started the fire."

"If your fool story was true," Hardin interjected, "Brutus would have been killed in the fire."

"They say a cat has nine lives, Hardin. Brutus came back to Stanton City with eight left. And that's what spooked you when you saw him there the day I rode in. Brutus, you supposed, had died in the C-C ranch-house, and you'd dismissed him from your mind, figuring that the finding of his bones wouldn't have aroused any suspicion. Most ranches have a cat or two around. But there Brutus was alive, and he was just like an accusing finger pointing at you. And when you went for your gun, you started Jake thinking. Jake hoped to make a little money off his notion, so Jake had to die. Saddling Jake's death on to me was killing two birds with one stone!"

"This is all crazy guesswork!"

Melody shrugged. "Maybe so. But remember this: It was me that found Brutus walking back to Stanton City and gave him a lift. I didn't know the Cinnibar then like I know it now. Otherwise I'd have right away seen the thing that got me to thinking later. You took Brutus out to the Quirt. Jake's wife can prove that. But when I found the tom-cat loping homeward, he wasn't coming from the direction of the Quirt. *He was coming from the C-C Connected.*"

Again Hardin ran his tongue along his lips. "McTeague talked?" he ventured. "You had McTeague long enough to get his clothes from him."

"McTeague's dead," Melody said. "You're alive. And you're going to fill in any missing pieces there are in my story."

Hardin managed to laugh. "And put my neck in a noose by doing it? Just try making me, mister!"

Very carefully Melody shook out the lariat he'd carried, and, just as carefully, he fashioned a noose in the end of the rope. This done, he dropped the noose over Hardin's head, tossed the rope over the lowest limb of the gnarled old tree beneath which they stood, and, catching the end of the rope, he fashioned a smaller noose in it, making a good hand hold for himself. Hardin watched all this in fascinated silence, and Melody said then, "Yes, I had McTeague for a while. Up on a canyon rim. I wanted to get a certain truth out of him, too. He taunted me for being too soft to really work him over. I've hardened up since then. The time has come to borrow a page out of your own book, Hardin. Do you talk — or do I hang you?"

"You wouldn't dare?"

"Knew a bald-complected professor fellow once. He told me a story about a gent called Achilles. Seems that when Achilles was a button, his maw dipped him in a certain creek, thereby giving him a cast-iron hide. But she had to hold him by the heel while she was dipping him, so his heel didn't get wet. That made one unprotected spot on him. The way the professor saw it, everybody has got his Achilles' heel. Yours is a fear of getting your neck stretched. That's another reason why you spooked when you saw Brutus. *Now talk, mister!*"

And now Melody hauled hard on the rope, taking the slack out of the lariat and drawing it taut. He had to put all his strength into the effort, but he had Hardin standing on tiptoes, the noose tightening to strangle the man; and when Melody eased up, Hardin choked for a long moment.

"Going to talk?" Melody demanded grimly. "Or shall I hoist you again?"

"*No!*" Hardin quavered and was reduced to a quivering hulk of terror-stricken flesh.

"Let go that rope! You figured it out right about Corday, and about Jake, too. But we only bashed Corday over the head and left him lying; we didn't put a bullet into him. McTeague and I did the job; and it was McTeague who killed Jake. Now will you ease up on that rope?"

With a gesture of disgust, Melody let go his end of the rope; and his disgust was that Hardin should have cracked so easily. Yet there was triumph in Melody, too; for the last piece had been fitted into the puzzle and now he knew everything he needed to know. He said, "We're going to find Sheriff Anse Crain now. And you're going to tell him this same story."

But suddenly Quirt Hardin was running, running clumsily with his hands still tied behind him but showing a great burst of speed for a man of his bulk, his intent obviously to bank everything on this one desperate play and elude Melody in the timber. The rope was still around Hardin's neck, and Melody snatched at the end of the lariat, but the rope was rising in the air, hauled upward as Hardin streaked away. The rope slithered over the limb and fell to the ground, and Melody went bounding after it.

What happened then, happened too quickly for Melody ever to have any coherent memory of the sequence of events. He was threshing through the brush, hard after the vanished Quirt owner; he heard the fat man's one wild, agonised yell — a yell that ended abruptly — and, stumbling to the lip of the cutbank where he'd recently looked down upon the range, Melody saw Hardin below him. The man had stumbled over the bank in his frantic flight, but his fall had been broken by the rope jerking taut. Hardin's boots were flailing as the man strangled before Melody's eyes. Melody got a hold on the rope and found that the small loop he'd fashioned at the other end had wedged between two rocks.

He didn't want Hardin dead. Hardin must tell his story to Sheriff Anse Crain before Melody could be cleared of the killing of Jake. So Melody jerked at the rope, his blind intent being to haul Hardin back to the lip of the cutbank. But the man's bulk was too much for Melody. Fumbling for McTeague's jackknife, Melody remembered the ivory-handled gun and got it out instead. He pressed the gun against the rope and fired; the smell of burning hemp choked him, but the rope parted. Sliding back to the edge of the cutbank, Melody looked downward, and, looking, shook his head. He'd been a moment too late. Quirt Hardin, whose Achilles' heel had been an unholy terror of hanging, had died with a noose around his neck.

Turning, Melody began clambering back up toward the brush, and in him was the bitter realisation that most of to-night's work had been in vain. And, climbing, he tripped over a root and fell. McTeague's gun, still in his hand, slipped away from him, and he groped for it and was at this task when a booted heel came down hard upon his wrist. Melody looked up to find a man towering over him.

Hardin, a few hours before, had claimed that one of his crew who had taken the trail to-day was a born tracker and had maintained that the man would keep on Melody's trail for ever. But it wasn't until this moment that Melody realised who Hardin had meant, for Curling Quirt's prize tracker was a former member of the crew who had lately rejoined the outfit. Melody hadn't seen him around the ranch this morning, but he knew the voice the instant the man spoke.

"By gar!" said Breed Lenoir. "Now I find you! This time we make one beeg fight and somebody die before she's finished. I come long ways back to keel you, my frien'."

Chapter XIX
Trouble's Troubadour

Otis Floren, heading out of Stanton City the night before, came most uncomfortably across the miles aboard a rented livery stable horse. He was on his way to carry Melody Malone's orders to the C-C Connected, and though the lawyer had made haste after that brief talk with Melody in his bedroom, Melody was far ahead of him this night, gone riding to bring about a promised miracle that would level the barrier which stood between the C-C herd and a cattle-buyer's bonus. Just how Melody was to bring this miracle about, Floren didn't know; and even Melody had seemed to have no concrete plan. Thus only an abiding faith lent spur to Floren to-night. He was doing his part, as instructed.

In any case, the showdown had come. This Floren sensed, and this too lent urgency to his heels as he belaboured the horse. Rocky Lynch had had his try at the fence and failed.

Sam Weaver had backed a bluff by heading his cattle southward, and Weaver, too, had failed. Now it was the C-C's turn. Yet the fence was still standing when Floren reached The Strip, and its tangible presence made a mute reminder that Quirt Hardin was still to be considered in the scheme of things; and the rifle in the hands of the sentry at the gate was eloquent of the means Hardin would employ if necessary.

The sentry let Floren pass unchallenged, though the Quirt hand's measured glance was far from welcoming; and at the second gate Floren was again allowed passage. The road took him southward to the fork which branched off, and here Floren turned in the direction of the Anvil and the Lazy-L. Had he continued toward the C-C, he might have met Melody wearing the clothing of Mc-Teague and trying to force speed out of a Curling Quirt horse that had recently hauled a dynamite-laden wagon.

But Floren's destination was the C-C roundup camp, and he chose to shorten the miles by striking overland. He knew roughly where he might expect to find the bedded gather; and in due time he saw the white tilts of the chuck-wagon and made out the vague blotch that was the herd and saw the dim movement of men riding endless circle. Most of the crew crawled beneath tarps, and among these mounded figures Floren found Dallas Spade. C-C's foreman woke at the lawyer's touch, propped himself upon an elbow and said, "What's up?"

"I sent word that a cattle-buyer was in town," Floren said. "Did you get the news?"

"I wasn't here when your man hit camp," Spade said. "I went south with Sam Weaver this morning. The pass is closed, Floren. We were expecting trouble, but we kept pushing forward anyway, figuring we'd hit cover if things looked wrong. We damned near got caught in an explosion, and Weaver had his cattle scattered all over creation. I didn't get back here until late. The boys told me the message you'd sent."

"I know all about what happened at the pass," Floren said. "Malone came to me tonight. That's why I'm here now. I've got orders for you, Spade. Malone wants you to start the herd toward Stanton City at dawn."

This fetched Spade upright in his blankets. "Is Malone crazy? We'd get no farther than The Strip. What are we supposed to do then? Pay the toll?"

"Malone says nobody will be blocking your way."

Spade shook his tousled, yellow head, crawled out of the blankets, found his boots and stamped into them. He glanced toward the east. "It won't be long until daylight. Malone's the boss. We'll move the herd. What happened to him at the Pass of the Blackrobes?"

Floren told him, then said, "Miss Corday at Weaver's place?"

Spade nodded. "I talked her into staying there while I went south, but she seems to think her place is at the C-C. I hope she doesn't go back alone."

"I'll go get her and take her back," Floren promised. "And I'll stay with her until you return with the crew. McTeague's still a prisoner at the C-C, unless Malone's moved him. You'll find the cattle-buyer at the Belle Fourche, Spade. You can collect from him in your capacity as foreman."

Spade smiled a bitter smile. "Providing we manage to reach Stanton City with the herd."

"Good luck!" Floren said and walked to his horse and laboriously climbed into the saddle. He headed in the direction of Sam Weaver's distant ranch-house, and Spade watched him go, keeping his eyes on the lawyer until Floren had disappeared. Spade's handsome face was a study; he stood lost in thought for many minutes, and then, with the first light beginning to show along the eastern hills, he began arousing his men. To them he gave brief orders, and if these stirred astonishment, they brought neither questions nor challenges from the C-C hands. Coffee was soon bubbling over a fire; the murkiness of this hour gave way to the grey dawn, but the sun had not yet shown itself when the time came to start.

Now there was all the confusion of getting under way. The chuck-wagon wouldn't be needed on a drive like this, for, if nothing untoward happened, the herd would be in Stanton City by sundown. So the cook was sent back to the home ranch. The bawling cattle, urged by popping rope-ends and lurid profanity, were strung out, the point fashioned into the likeness of a blunt arrowhead aimed northward; and up in the lead Dallas Spade took his place. Other riders rode at flank and swing, keeping the cattle bunched together; to the rear came the drag riders, eating the dusts of thousands of hooves, turning back such recalcitrant cattle as showed a penchant for wandering.

And now they were on the move, heading northward, going slowly, for a steer's natural gait is slow, and Dallas Spade, always careful with cattle, intended to keep the tallow on them. More than that, he rode with no sense of urgency, no enthusiasm for to-day's doings. He had his orders, and, he was carrying them out. But when they reached the fence, there'd be a sentry posted — a sentry whose ready rifle could send a signal that would fetch Hardin's patrolling riders. Of this Spade was certain, and therefore he saw no sense in hurrying. Floren's kind of faith hadn't been contagious.

Thus they plodded along through the morning; the sun lifted above the hills, showering its gold down upon the range; behind Spade the cattle trailed, a bawling, twining, dusty queue; and the crew did its monotonous work. The miles unreeled; they reached the road that pointed toward Stanton City; they paralleled this road and came past the ridge where Spade and Anita had once cowered in helplessness, watching as Quirt Hardin's crew escorted Melody toward a hangtree. Soon the fence was in sight, the fence and the gates, and Spade came alive with interest then, his eyes widening; for no man lolled beyond that gate.

Even then Spade refused to accept the truth; his thought was that perhaps the sentry had absented himself just for a few minutes and might be skylined at any moment. Or perhaps this was some trap of Quirt Hardin's, some ruse to force a showdown that had been too long delayed for the man's liking. But when he reached the fence, Spade came down out of his saddle, opened the gate and hauled it aside, mounted again and pointed the way across The Strip. Behind him now his crew sweated, forcing the long queue of cattle down to a narrowness that would permit easy passage. And before the last of the cattle were through that south gate, Spade was in sight of the north gate; and it, too, was deserted.

Again he left the gate open behind him, and now he sat his saddle at one side, waiting as the cattle came through. His eyes questing all the directions, he saw no rider, though dimly, far, far to the west, he thought he made out swirling dust that might have been raised by distant horsemen. Yet the longer he studied that tiny banner, the more he became convinced that whoever the riders were, they were heading away, heading toward the western Cinnibar Hills.

Spade shook his head. The last of the C-C cattle had crossed The Strip; the last rider was dismounting to close the gate behind them, obeying a rangeland edict with a careful courtesy that was all too ironic. Spade aroused himself, touched spurs to his horse, and was soon back in point position.

Now they had only to toil onward, toil toward Stanton City; and there was no fence to bar the way, no man with legal right to challenge their passage. Somehow, incredibly, The Strip had been left unguarded. Somehow the miracle had been wrought.

Melody Malone, then, had known what he was talking about when he'd sent Otis Floren with instructions to have the herd moved to town. Malone had conceived a plan and put it through. Malone had succeeded in besting Quirt Hardin — succeeded where Rocky Lynch and Sam Weaver, each in his separate way, had failed. And, considering all this, Spade knew now that Melody would batter down any obstacle when he put his mind to it. And so, at long last, Spade sensed the reason for the faith that had prompted Otis Floren to name Melody as Chance Corday's heir, for Spade had now seen that faith justified. Melody Malone had proved his right to the ownership of the C-C Connected to-day — proved it beyond dispute.

And where did that leave Dallas Spade? C-C's foreman knew the answer all too well. The game had played itself out for him on the Cinnibar; his sun had set the day Malone had ridden into Stanton City. That would have put the hate in some men, but not in Dallas Spade. When one page was turned, you put it behind you and looked to the next. He'd dreamed a dream on Cinnibar Range, had Spade; that dream had burned to ashes. But there was yet the shape of one last opportunity.

Ahead the road stretched toward Stanton

City, a dusty ribbon in the strong sunlight. But Dallas Spade was seeing a forked trail, and the choice was his. And now he knew which fork he'd be taking. . . .

Melody Malone, deep in the Cinnibar Hills that night, faced no such choice of procedure. Clambering up the cutbank after Quirt Hardin's death and finding Breed Lenoir awaiting him, a challenge on the man's lips, Melody knew he must fight for his life. He'd bested this huge hulk once, but that had been another time and another fight; and the advantage was Lenoir's now. His heel upon Melody's wrist, Lenoir was drawing a knife. Moonlight, filtering through the tree tops, touched the blade as Lenoir sent it lunging downward.

But Lenoir, in wielding the knife, instinctively leaned forward, thus throwing his weight to the balls of his feet, and this took the pressure of his boot heel off Melody's wrist. Melody, freed, didn't try groping for McTeague's lost gun. There wasn't time for that. Instead he wrapped his arms around Lenoir's knees and reared upward, hoisting Lenoir from the ground. His plan was to catapult Lenoir over his head, but the pitch of the slope precluded that; Melody, in coming erect, leaned too far backwards; the weight of Lenoir bowled him over, and the two went down the slope together.

They ended up below Hardin's body, a writhing, twisting tangle of arms and legs; and they went rolling, Lenoir trying for a hold on Melody's throat with his free hand, Melody striving desperately to get a grip on the wrist of the hand that held the knife. Somewhere in the midst of that struggle, he felt the bite of the knife; fire ran along his upper left arm, and the blood came. Melody lost his grip then, and Lenoir got a hold on the troubadour's throat. Moonlight danced on the knife blade once again as Lenoir raised it aloft.

That was when Melody pinned all his strength to one last effort. His back was to the ground, but he succeeded in rolling over in spite of Lenoir's weight upon him, and he made another try at Lenoir's right wrist, not knowing whether his own wounded arm would do his will. But he stopped that descending blade, and he turned the knife aside as he rolled. He was twisting frantically at Lenoir's wrist, hoping to force the man to drop the knife, yet knowing that Lenoir doubtless had another knife in the neck scabbard sewed inside his shirt collar. He got Lenoir beneath him and tried battering at the man with his free fist, but suddenly Lenoir had gone limp.

It wasn't until Melody had torn himself

away and got to a stand that he understood what had happened. He'd turned the knife blade aside, and, in turning it, the blade had been pointed toward Lenoir. And somewhere in that last, desperate struggling, the blade had been driven home by the pressure of their writhing bodies.

Pawing the sweat from his eyes, Melody began clambering up the slope again, and it was when he reached its crest that he found another man shaped up out of the night. One of the Quirt's Crew, he supposed, and despair swept over him, for he was still unarmed and his bout with Breed Lenoir and the wound he'd thus received had sapped him. But he lunged forward; again there was no choice, and he'd almost closed with this man when the fellow spoke. "That you, Malone?" the man asked, and relief threatened to unhinge Melody's knees, for it was the voice of Sheriff Anse Crain.

"Sorry," Melody muttered and wondered if he were going to faint. "Sorry . . . about that clout I gave you . . . in the jail."

Crain said, "That don't matter. Not now. What's the matter with your left arm? Let's have a look."

Melody obediently stripped off McTeague's coat and shirt, and Crain, peering hard in the moonlight, said, "Nothing to worry about unless you keep on losing blood. Wait till I skin out of my undershirt and I'll make a bandage for you."

"What fetched you here?" Melody asked weakly as Crain fumbled at shirt buttons.

"You, you crazy galoot," Crain said. "I've been trailing you ever since Otis Floren let me out of my own handcuffs. To-day the sign showed that half of the Cinnibar was riding west. I tagged along. These hills are swarming with Quirt hands, but I'm not too much worried about them. Another sun-up will see them heading out of the country. They'll hit the grit once they learn that the paymaster is dead."

"You know about Hardin?"

Crain tore a strip from his undershirt, the cloth glimmering whitely. "I watched your little necktie party from the brush. Wanted to see what come of it before I showed my hand. Then, when Hardin made his break and you lit out after him, I followed. Lenoir showed up just about then. He must have guessed that whatever had fetched me into the hills, it wasn't to side with Quirt. He swiped at me with his gun-barrel and left me lying. It was you he was after. I got to my feet just in time to see the last of the fracas. How's that? Bandage too tight?"

But Melody wasn't concerned with Anse

Crain's crude but effective ministrations. Not now. "Let me get this straight," Melody said breathlessly. "You were in the brush while I worked on Hardin? You mean you heard what he said — about how Chance Corday died? And Jake?"

Crain nodded. "That's why I ain't holding it against you for clouting me. Looks like you got yourself out of the pokey to do my work. Feel like you could sit a saddle?"

"I feel like you could put the saddle on me and I'd pack you and the horse home!" Melody said jubilantly. "Let's get riding."

"There's a burying job to be done hereabouts," Crain observed. "But I'll send somebody out from town later to pick up Hardin and Lenoir."

Crain's horse was not far away, and though it didn't take kindly to being double-burdened, it suffered this indignity with passable grace after a first few hectic moments. They came down out of the hills unchallenged, and this, in itself, was the proof that Breed Lenoir had been the real tracker of the Quirt outfit. Wherever the other Quirt hands were now keeping themselves, it apparently wasn't in this vicinity. And Melody, like Anse Crain, soon dismissed them from his mind. Those men were like the fence that had worried every one. With Quirt Hardin gone, all obstacles to peace on the Cinnibar were gone. Yet Melody was in a hurry to reach the C-C, and said so.

"We'll get you there," Crain promised him. "But what's your rush? Your work is sure as shootin' all done *this* fall."

But Melody, remembering that there was still a thing or two Anse Crain couldn't possibly know, had a different feeling. There was one last chore yet to be done, one last showdown to be faced. And until the finish, he was still trouble's troubadour, consigned by his own code to see things through.

Light blazed in the C-C ranch-house when they finally looked upon it; and horses milled in the corral; and there was more sign of activity than Melody had ever witnessed about the place. The two got stiffly down from the horse, and when they tramped to the door, Anita admitted them with a glad cry. Otis Floren was here, and a good many C-C hands crowded the house as well.

Floren crossed quickly to Melody and took his hand and said, "I don't know how you did it, my boy, but you did. No one challenged the herd at The Strip. The cattle were duly delivered to Stanton City, and the bonus belongs to the C-C."

Melody said, "Where's Spade?"

One of the C-C hands answered. "That's what we're all beginning to wonder," he said.

"When we got to town and delivered the cows to the shipping pens, Spade told us he was going to the Belle Fourche to collect the cash. Likewise he told us to ride on home when we were ready, just in case business tied him up. But we all had us a drink or two before we left, and we figgered Spade would be back here ahead of us. That was a couple of hours ago, and he ain't showed yet. You don't suppose somebody jumped him along the road for that money he'd 'a' been totin'?"

The old grimness, the grimness that had first manifested itself in Stanton's jail, returned to Melody, and he said, "You've all got questions to ask. The sheriff, here, can answer them for you. I've got to ride to town. Now!"

He went out of the house with Anita calling his name after him; he closed the door upon a babble of questions and ejaculations and got to the corral and laid a loop on his own horse. His wounded arm was stiff, but other than that it didn't bother him. He retrieved his guitar from the bunkhouse and almost instinctively slung it across his back. But what he was really looking for was his gun, until he remembered that McTeague had probably fetched it to the Quirt this morning, when McTeague had died. But Melody found another gun, one which might have belonged to any of the C-C crew. It might even have been Dallas Spade's gun — a spare the foreman had discarded for a newer weapon. There was no telling.

It didn't matter. The trail pointed to Stanton City and the last showdown; and Melody was ready now.

Chapter XX
The Last Showdown

The Strip lay dark and deserted when Melody reached it, and there was no gate to bar the way. The gate had been torn from its fastenings, and, when Melody approached the far fence, its gate, too, was gone. Melody needed no explanation for this. The C-C hands had delivered a herd to town to-day, tarried for a drink or two, then ridden home, tired but triumphant. On the return trip their exuberant spirit had manifested itself in this manner; ready lariats and hard-pulling horses had hauled the gates away; and this show of contempt was symbolic. In due time all of Hardin's fence would be destroyed, and no man would ever rear another barrier against his neighbours on Cinnibar range.

Few lights showed in Stanton City when Melody sighted the town. The night was far gone; he'd ridden many miles since sundown, and weariness was beginning to tell on him again. He drew some consolation from the thought that soon the last job would be done, and he promised himself that he would then find the most comfortable bunk on C-C's premises and sleep an eternity or two. When he rode into the main street, he saw saddlers still standing at the hitch-rails of a couple of the saloons, and a few lights showed in the windows of the Belle Fourche. But the real activity was down at the railroad yards, and even this had dwindled to almost nothing. Melody headed toward the tangle of tracks.

The herd which had been delivered to Stanton City hours earlier had since been loaded into stock cars. These cars stood out vaguely against the night; the bawling of the penned, nervous cattle made a constant discordance; and Melody, swinging down from his saddle in the shadow of the depot's eaves, saw a bobbing lantern or two and the dim movement of men, and he also saw that the men were converging upon a day coach, which, along with the caboose, tagged the long line of stock cars. Up ahead, a locomotive chuffed. This train would shortly be departing eastward.

Guesswork had guided Melody here. If a man wanted to leave Stanton City hastily tonight, that man would be wise to choose the stock train as his means of departure. Whatever pursuit might come would be by saddle-horse, and the train would give the fugitive the advantage. True, the train would also be carrying the cattle-buyer's stock-tending crew, and possibly the buyer himself, and these men, or the train crew, might discover a stranger aboard. But if the stranger were careful to keep out of sight until the train was ready to leave and crews were in coach and caboose, that stranger would be reasonably safe. Then, with a margin of safety between himself and Stanton City, the stock train stowaway could get off at another town, buy or steal a horse, and vanish completely from the sight and the knowledge of Cinnibar Range.

Thus Melody, putting himself into another man's boots, had reasoned as this other man might have reasoned. And he'd arrived here with few minutes to spare, for the train was about ready to depart. And, darting from the shadow of one of the loading pens and heading toward the train, came a man with a small carpet-bag in his left hand. It took little deduction to realise that this bag contained the money the cattle-buyer had paid for C-C's cattle. From the ease with which the bag was handled, Melody judged that it contained currency — Eastern money.

Melody's quick striding fetched him after the man, and when he was almost to the fugitive's elbow, he said, "Just a minute, Spade."

Dallas Spade swung around, surprise on his handsome face, and he said, "*You — !*"

"Why not?" Melody countered. "It's C-C's money, and I'm C-C's boss."

Spade said, "Your face shows what you're thinking, Malone. You're dead wrong. Yes, this is the money. But the reason I'm here is that I wanted to see the cattle-buyer again before he left, and I reckon he's with his crew. Forgot to ask him about next year's business. No reason C-C shouldn't fill his wants."

"No reason at all, Spade. But your story's thin. You were set to quit the country."

"And throw away the foremanship of the C-C and turn outlaw in the bargain? Why would I do that — even for this money? Chance Corday's will said I was to have the job as long as I wanted it."

"That would hold some men," Melody said. "But not you, Spade. Being a foreman was just a starter for you. You wouldn't sink down your roots on any range where you couldn't climb any higher than that. And I'm the man who chokes your chances."

Spade smiled then, smiled and shrugged. "You're smart, Malone. Far smarter than I figured you to be. That was my mistake. But a ranch isn't to your liking; you're too much of a tumbleweed to stay put long. Let's take the trail together. We'd make a real team, the pair of us. And, for a starter, we'll split what's in this bag. You figure that doesn't make sense, eh? You're thinking that everything in the bag can be yours anyway, as boss of the C-C. But what I'm offering you is a partnership. Trail with me and we'll fill this bag many times."

Melody shook his head, a vast disgust in his face. "Once I'd have been proud to call you partner, Spade. You've got brains, and you've got guts. But you've likewise got blood on your hands, mister — dirty, bushwhacking blood. And that's what fetched me on your trail to-night. I put a rope around one killer's neck since sundown. It will pleasure me to turn another over to Sheriff Anse Crain."

Spade stiffened, then said, "What in blazes are you talking about?"

"Chance Corday, Spade. Quirt Hardin is dead, but before he died he talked. Hardin planned a pat scheme to get rid of Corday. He came to the C-C, knocked Corday over the head, then fixed things so the ranch-house would catch fire *after* Hardin had left. It worked out that way, but you rode in from round-up camp that night and saw the blaze. You once told me you tried to reach Corday. You did reach him, too. There must have been a lot of men in Corday. In spite of the clout Hardin had given him, Corday was alive — alive enough to have started crawling out of that burning house. Or so I guess. In any case, you finished what Hardin had started. You put a bullet through Corday's head and left him to burn, figuring there wouldn't be enough left of Corday to show how he'd died. But, to keep up appearances, seeing as the crew knew you'd gone to the home-ranch, you rode after the hands and fetched them back to form a bucket-brigade."

Spade cleared his throat twice before he said, "What kind of crazy guesswork is this? Hardin must have planted such a notion with you, and Hardin couldn't have known anything I did that night — not if Hardin cleared out before the fire, like you said."

"Hardin gave me only one piece to the puzzle, Spade. Hardin denied putting a bullet into Corday, though he admitted everything else. Which shows Hardin wasn't lying. Yet Doc Bishop looked at Corday's body the other morning and found a bullet in him. *There isn't anybody else in the world who had a chance to trigger that bullet but you!*"

"And you figure I did *that* to Chance Corday?"

"And for a good reason — from your point of view, Spade. No man ever counted much with you — except yourself. The night you shot Corday, you thought his will named you as heir. Yes, Floren told me about Corday's first will — told me not long ago in the Stanton jail when I was trying to get the whole picture of this range and its people. Waiting for Chance Corday to die was too slow for you. Killing him under ordinary circumstances was too risky. But Hardin, without meaning to do so, had dealt you what seemed a pat hand. You had your choice the night of the fire — to drag Corday out of the house and go on being his foreman, or to finish him off for sure and own the ranch."

Whether the hate had been latent in Dallas Spade these many days since Melody Malone's coming, or whether it was born full-bodied at this very moment, possibly Spade himself could not have told. But suddenly the hate was naked in his eyes, and his free right hand swept downward to his hip, and his gun came out of leather and gave blossom to a spiteful red flower in the darkness. Melody, swerving aside and trying for his own gun, went off balance and came down upon one knee. Spade could have finished him then, but the train whistle had shrieked hoarsely, blanketing the sound of gun-fire, and Spade turned and darted off in the darkness, darted toward the train.

Melody went after him at a hard run, then paused, his eyes questing the shadows for sight of the fugitive. When he saw Spade, the man was climbing the ladder of one of the stock cars, clambering frantically toward the roof, and even though he was encumbered by the carpet-bag, he swarmed upward with remarkable agility. And Melody, snapping a shot and knowing that he'd missed, followed after the man. He got to the stock car just as the locomotive, far up ahead, hissed steam; and then he was climbing after Spade. Melody was clutching his gun, and this was a handicap in the ascent, and his wounded left arm was stiff and sore; but his agility matched Spade's. He got to the top of the car and saw Spade fleeing along the catwalk. Spade turned, and, seeing Melody coming, fired again, the bullet plucking at Melody's sleeve. The train whistle sounded; and Melody lifted his gun and triggered once more.

What damage that bullet did, Melody was never to know. It was a hit, for Spade flung up his arms, releasing his grip on the carpet-bag, and the bag flew outward and fell to the side of the track. But at this moment the train lurched violently, the couplings jarring, and Spade staggered with the unexpected motion. He'd reached the end of the car and had been about to leap to the next car, but now he spun frantically around. His eyes were open, and hate and a great panic were in them. Then, before Melody's horrified gaze, Spade fell. The man tried vainly to grasp at a brake wheel, and, missing, disappeared between the two cars. The train was in motion as Melody got to the ladder and came down it, and the ground was blurring past when he reached the last rung and leaped.

He lighted on his feet, stumbled, pitched headlong, and he came erect as the caboose flashed by; and then there was only its red tail-light to be seen. He went back along the track, his eyes bent to the ground, and he saw a shapeless something between the rails and shuddered and averted his eyes. Within a few feet of that stop, he stumbled upon the carpet-bag. He lifted it from the ground and found Otis Floren standing a few paces away and gazing at him. The lawyer's face looked haggard in the last starlight.

"So you finished all the chores," Floren said.

"You knew? "Melody asked. "You knew about Spade?"

Floren shook his head. "Not for sure. The man was efficient, and he showed a loyalty to his salt, but there was always a metallic hardness beneath the surface, and that made me wonder. Yet even to-night, when he failed to show back at the ranch with the money,

I was no more suspicious than was the crew. But when you lit out for Stanton City, I guessed why you were going. And I followed you."

Melody said, "Hardin confessed everything. Anse Crain heard him, and Crain can tell you the story. The bullet Doc Bishop found in Corday wasn't put there by Hardin. Does that tell you all you need to know?"

Floren nodded. "Add that to Spade's own story of the night of the fire, and the picture is complete. You won't have to answer to Anse Crain for what is lying yonder on the track."

Melody said, "We'll have to have his body taken care of. And then this money must be toted to the C-C."

"And after that, Melody?"

The troubadour shrugged. "I'm stuck with a ranch, I guess. I'll try to do a proper job of running it. Lucky I've got a good crew. I should be able to get along with them now that they've found I'm not as useless as I look."

Something was working in Floren's face, something that seemed to choke him up and make words hard come by, and Melody, seeing this, said softly, "There's something more on your mind, eh? Speak up, Floren."

Floren's eyes were grateful. "There had to be a time when I'd tell you this, Melody. That time has come. I've tried to be a good lawyer and to serve my clients in an honest fashion. That's why, when Quirt Hardin's scheme became apparent, all three of the big south range ranchers turned to me. And that's when I began to wonder what good a row of law books was against Hardin. Chance Corday also saw that stronger armament was needed."

"So Corday changed his will."

"Corday's will gave the C-C to Dallas Spade. I drew up that will, months ago. Then Corday discovered he had a niece, and, blood being thicker than water, he decided to change his will. We talked about the girl, and that was when Corday began to wonder if he would only be willing the girl a mess of trouble — a fight too big for her to handle. And he told me then that he wasn't sure about Dallas Spade. Spade had nerve, but not the kind to buck Hardin. Corday wondered if a will would stand the test of the courts if it gave the C-C to a stranger — any stranger who proved himself big enough to buck Hardin."

"And that's how the new will came to be drawn up?"

"That's how the notion got started, Melody. But Chance Corday died too soon. I *drew* up that second will. And I forged Corday's name to it, and the names of witnesses, a couple of ranchers who had just moved out of the

Cinnibar. I was carrying out the plan that Corday hadn't lived to complete. It was Corday's *will* in the true sense of the word. But that will nevertheless, has no legal standing."

Melody began to laugh, and he was tired enough that his laughter had an edge of hysteria to it. "Then the legal owner of the C-C is lying yonder on the tracks."

"The showdown with Hardin was bound to have proved Spade's real standing, one way or another," Floren said. "Had he stacked up as worthy, I'd have laid the truth before you and asked for your mercy. Even though it meant exposing myself as a forger. But what can we do now?"

Melody lifted a friendly hand to Floren's high shoulder. "A bald-complected professor fellow told me that every man at one time or another compromises with his conscience. Those were the very words he used. Most men turn the trick for their own gain — like Dallas Spade figured on doing. You're the only man I ever heard of who strayed from the path for somebody else's sake rather than your own. You were loyal to Chance Corday, even after he was dead. You've got no problem, mister. The ranch belongs to Anita. That was Chance Corday's real wish. He wanted it hers, but he wanted peace on the range when she took over. Things are squared around now."

"But how do we straighten out the mess I made, Melody?"

"Once I wrote a note giving the ranch to Anita. That note still holds. When I ride away, she's got no choice but to accept the gift. That makes me out to be pretty noble, Floren, but you and I will always know different. I'll just be giving her back what's rightfully hers."

"I've got your note in my desk. It's legal enough. But it makes a poor showing for you, Malone. You earned the ranch. Now you'll be turning your back on it."

Melody shook his head. "I've lost nothing. I'll be leaving this town with everything I had when I rode into it. That's fair enough."

Floren got an extravagant bandanna and lustily blew his long nose. "You'll be leaving with much more than you fetched in," he said. "You'll be leaving with the gratitude of all of us, of myself and the ranchers and Mrs. Jake and Anse Crain. You'll be leaving it a place worth living in. You'll be a long time remembered, Melody."

"That's something," Melody conceded and pressed the carpet-bag into Floren's hand. "Will you see that Spade's body is moved?"

"But what will I tell Anita about you?" Floren asked with concern. "She likes you, Melody; I've seen that. How am I going to explain why you rode off without even saying good-bye?"

"Tell her that I'm a tumbleweed and I've felt the tug of the wind. Tell her I had one more hill to climb, one more town to see. She'll savvy. So long, Floren. I've got my horse over by the depot. I'll bed on the prairie to-night."

He felt Floren's hand groping for his; he felt the pressure of the lawyer's fingers; and he remembered the first time he'd shaken hands with the lawyer. There was a new strength in Floren now. And then Melody went wandering into the shadows, heading for his horse, his guitar bouncing against his back, his gun restored to its holster. The work was done.

Chapter XXI
One More Town

Horsehoof had been Horsehoof, a town grown from the naked prairie and content to bloom like any other desert flower, unhonoured and unsung, until Stanton City, thirty miles to the west, had blossomed belatedly into being. Whereupon Horsehoof's tobacco-chewing equivalent of a Chamber of Commerce had met in solemn, if somewhat whisky-besotted, conclave and decreed that herewith and hereafter the establishment heretofore known as Horsehoof would be called Garden City, and that, furthermore, any absent-minded or unpatriotic galoot who inadvertently used the former name would be publicly stretched over a rain-barrel and beaten with a pair of chaps, dunked in the town horse-trough, and run down the road till his pockets were dipping sand.

Into this sorry collection of false-fronts rode Melody Malone on a sunny afternoon, looking like any other saddle tramp except that a silver-plated guitar was slung across his back. To such meagre curiosity as was displayed over his coming, Melody remained immune. He came down from his saddle before a livery stable, routed out the hostler and said, "Grain my horse, feller."

The hostler ran his eyes over Melody's lanky length, taking in the remnants of the garments that had once been McTeague's, and this custodian of oats and hay said, "Got a dollar on you?"

Melody silently began fishing for the dollar, and, after diligent effort, succeeded in placing a sufficiency of small coins in the hostler's ready palm. Whereupon Melody asked, "Got a good restaurant here?"

"Most folks favour Joe's Steak House over yonder," the hostler said, the sweep of his arm indicating the direction. "It's run by a brother-in-law of mine."

Melody nodded, lifted his sombrero and ran his fingers through his thick, brown thatch, set the hat at a take-it-or-leave-it angle and headed across the street, his guitar bouncing against him. His step was jaunty, yet there was a certain bleakness in his eyes that hadn't been there when he'd viewed other towns. He knew now that some part of his enthusiasm was gone, and it came to him quite suddenly, and quite disconcertingly, that when you'd seen one town, you'd seen them all. But a man still had to make himself a living, and, with Garden City's loiterers watching him with lethargic curiosity, he came to the chewed hitch-rail before Joe's Steak House.

The restaurant was a frame building, and affixed to its wide, unwashed window was a sign so old that the sun had yellowed it and dimmed the printing almost to oblivion. This sign read: TO-DAY'S SPECIAL — STEAK! Perching himself upon the hitch-rail, Melody got the guitar into his hands, plucked a chord, and began singing:

"I know a gal on Chowder Crick,
Sassy as a squirrel and fatter'n a tick,
Hi, yo, diddle, di, day. . . .
Her teeth come out at the sunset hour
Her complexion's the colour of a sack of flour,
One look from her and the cream goes sour.
Hi, yo diddle, di, da-a-a-y. . . .

"Yup, I know a gal on Chowder Crick,
Homely as a hedge-fence, duller that a stick,
Hi, yo, diddle, di, day. . . .
But her pappy's rigged with a gold mine claim,

And me I could use a little of the same,
So I'm gettin' fixed to marry up with that dame.
Hi, yo, diddle, di, da-a-a-y. . . ."

Faces pressed themselves against the restaurant window and men loomed in the doorway, and Melody lifted his voice even higher:

"Got me a rival on Chowder Creek,
Eight feet tall in his stocking feet,
Hi, yo, diddle, di, day. . . .
And this big galoot comes a-courtin' too,
All decked out like a gol-darned Sioux,
Looks like I bit off more'n I can chew,
Hi, yo, diddle, di, da-a-a-y. . . ."

Loiterers, sunning themselves at the edge of the boardwalks or keeping to the shade of the wooden awnings of various establishments, began drifting toward the restaurant, forming a silent, appreciative, grinning audience. Melody gave the guitar an extra-special twang.

"I'm diggin' me a bear trap on Chowder Creek,
Aim to ketch a grizzly that walks on two feet,
Hi, yo, diddle, di, day. . . .

And when my rival comes a-courtin'
  Maisie,
He's in for a fall that'll shake him up
  crazy,
'Cause, that trap's in the trail, and she's
  sure a daisy,
Hi, yo, diddle, di, da-a-a-y. . . ."

Melody grinned back at the growing audience, debated as to how much he should thus freely dispense before approaching Joe of the Steak House on the subject of a man's singing for his supper, and then added one more verse:

"Now hell's sure a-poppin' on Chowder
  Creek,
And I'm shakin' the dust of that range
  off my feet,
Hi, yo, diddle, di, day. . . .
My bear trap worked like a fancy charm,
Caught me a man; didn't do him much
  harm,
But it was Maisie's *paw,* and he busted
  his arm,
Hi, yo, diddle, di, da-a-a-y. . . ."

Sliding off the hitch-rail, Melody slung the guitar over his shoulder and stepped toward the restaurant door. But at this point a big and burly man, black of brow and formidable of appearance, detached himself from Melody's audience and strode forward. The bulk of him blocked Melody's way and the afternoon sunlight caught the high glint of a sheriff's ball-pointed star upon the big man's vest. This lawman said, "Reckon you'd be him, all right."

"Well," said Melody. "I always have been. What's troubling you, Sheriff?"

The lawman reached and plucked the gun from Melody's holster, showing considerable alacrity for a man of his girth, and, prodding Melody's gun into the troubadour's ribs, said, "Better come along peaceable. The jail house is just a step down the street."

"And what in blazes am I being jailed for?" Melody demanded.

But the sheriff gave him no answer. Herding Melody ahead of him, he escorted the troubadour to a log and frame building which might have been a twin to the Stanton City calaboose, ushered him through an office and down a cell corridor, and in no time at all a barred door was clanging in Melody's face.

"Just make yourself as comfortable as you can," the sheriff said. "Reckon you've been in jail before."

"So much lately that it's getting monotonous," Melody admitted. "Are you telling me why I'm decorating this pokey?"

For answer the sheriff strode toward his office, returning a moment later with a flimsy bit of yellow paper which he thrust between the bars. Melody saw that it was a telegram, sent over the wires that paralleled the railroad out of Stanton City to the east and the west. The wire read:

BE ON THE LOOK-OUT FOR CHARACTER TOTING A GUITAR AND SINGING SONG ABOUT A GAL ON CHOWDER CRICK STOP THIS SCOUNDREL WANTED HERE FOR STEALING VALUABLE SILVER-PLATED GUITAR WHICH WAS PROPERTY OF ANITA CORDAY STOP PLEASE HOLD PRISONER AND ADVISE US STOP TREAT HIM GENTLE BUT FIRM AS CHARACTER IS DESPERATE WHEN FULLY AROUSED.

SHERIFF ANSE CRAIN

Melody flung the paper back at the lawman. "This is Crazy!" Melody cried. "The guitar belongs to me. It's always belonged to me, and it's always going to belong to me."

"You got papers to prove it, young feller?"

"Papers — ? Of course I haven't got papers! It's a guitar, not a horse I'm supposed to have stolen. This is a trick, rigged up by Anita Corday and helped along by Anse Crain. You see, Sheriff, I owned a valuable ranch on the

Cinnibar, and I gave it to the Corday girl. She don't want to accept the gift, so she's thrown out a loop for me so I'll be held till she can give the ranch back."

The sheriff took a hasty backward step. "Sure, sure," he said soothingly. "That's probably the straight of it. You go around giving away ranches, but people just naturally don't want them. I'm wiring Crain. Likely he'll be in on to-night's train to identify you and the guitar. Meanwhile you're staying right where you are. You ought to be ashamed. A fully-grown man stealing a guitar from a lady!"

"Why, listen, you walnut-headed, limb-brained, over-stuffed excuse for a star-toter. If I — !"

But the sheriff of Garden City was gone from the corridor and only the echo of his ringing boots remained. Melody slumped down upon a stool, realising that there was nothing to do but resign himself, and here he sat while the afternoon drifted away and the night came.

The sheriff put in an appearance then, fetching food for Melody, and it was the troubadour's reflection that at least he'd got one of Joe's steaks without having had to sing for it. But the sheriff had no answers to Melody's questions, and no ear for Melody's protestations of innocence, and there was nothing for Melody to do afterwards but watch the buzzing winged creatures which fluttered about the overhanging lamp the sheriff had lighted out in the corridor.

It was nearly midnight when Melody heard the train whistle; it was ten minutes later that Anita walked into the corridor. She wore the blue, tailored suit in which he had first seen her, and when he looked at her now, anger was in him, but so, too, was a gladness and a longing. She grinned at Melody through the bars and said, "I've already told the sheriff that I'm convinced that you're the scoundrel who stole my guitar. But I've agreed to press no charges if he'll release you into my custody. You'll be free only on probation, you understand."

Melody said darkly, "If this door was unlocked — !"

The gayness went out of Anita, and she said, "Why did you ride away, Melody? I know everything now — the truth about Dallas Spade, and about Uncle Chauncey's original will. Otis Floren's conscience couldn't stand the load it was carrying. But nothing had changed really. You were still the man who earned the C-C Connected."

Melody said, "One part of that is right, Anita. Nothing changed. Dallas Spade saw it straight when he claimed that you should own the C-C. Reckon he had plans for getting hold of it, once it was in your hands, but the real point is that the ranch belongs to you. I want it left that way."

"And you, Melody — ?"

He shrugged. "I'm a tumbleweed."

"Isn't there room enough on the C-C for you to do your rolling? Now that Hardin's gone, the Quirt acreage will be up for sale. We could buy it too, if you're crowded. I'm sure that C-C's new owner wouldn't object to our expanding."

"C-C's *new* owner?"

Anita smiled. "It was the only way I could see to get round that stubborn pride of yours. Otis Floren seems to specialise in crazy wills and queer bits of legal procedure. I've asked him to have the C-C deeded to an outsider with provisions that you and I, Melody, are to run it as joint-managers for the owner. Would you come back on that basis — as a partner of mine?"

"You mean we'd run the spread for somebody else? But who's the owner?"

"Why, Brutus, that big, one-eyed, yellow tom-cat," Anita replied. "If Uncle Chauncey could will a ranch to a man he never saw, surely I can deed the same ranch to a tom-cat. After all, it was Brutus who put you on the trail of Quirt Hardin, according to Anse Crain.

You wouldn't object to working for Brutus, would you?"

He began to laugh, heartily and without restraint, and she laughed too; and, just as Dallas Spade had once sensed that there was a real kinship between Melody and Anita, so Melody now sensed this closeness. Anita must have guessed the run of his thoughts, for she said, softly, "You did a good job of putting the pieces of a puzzle together, Melody. Did you overlook one? Didn't you understand why Dallas Spade chose to run away with the cattle money that last day? Dallas had seen the way I looked at you the night you headed for the Pass of the Blackrobes to stop Hardin's dynamiters. He knew then that no matter what happened, there'd be no chance of his marrying me to get the C-C. He knew that I'd given my heart away."

Melody came close to the bars and reached out for her. "The ranch never meant much to me," he said soberly. "I fought one fight because Quirt Hardin had made it personal, but I had a different reason for taking Spade's trail that last night. Chance Corday was *your* kin. Somebody had to square up for him."

She said, "Then you didn't really leave because you had one more hill to climb, one more town to see."

He said, "Whenever I looked for a new

town, I was looking for something, only I didn't know what it was. Not until I found it in Stanton City. Wherever you are will be the place where I'll be satisfied to sink down roots."

She produced a key from the folds of her skirt and held it up for him to see. "The sheriff gave me this when I told him the whole truth," she said. "Those telegrams which Anse Crain sent to the sheriffs in every direction out of Stanton City were the only thing I could think of to have you stopped. Is it safe for me to open your cell door now?"

"That all depends on the way you look at it," said Melody.

The key grated and the door creaked upon its hinges, and after that there was no more said, and no more need for words. They were into each other's arms, and their lips met and clung, and in this manner the partnership was sealed. It was all of ten minutes later that the sheriff of Garden City, looking into the cell corridor, quietly pulled the door shut behind him and tiptoed from his office and out into the street, grinning as wide as a man could grin.

The employees of THORNDIKE PRESS hope you have enjoyed this Large Print book. All our Large Print books are designed for easy reading — and they're made to last.

Other Thorndike Large Print books are available at your library, through selected bookstores, or directly from us. Suggestions for books you would like to see in Large Print are always welcome.

For more information about current and upcoming titles, please call or mail your name and address to:

THORNDIKE PRESS
PO Box 159
Thorndike, Maine 04986
800/223-6121
207/948-2962

ST. CROIX FALLS PUBLIC LIBRARY
ST. CROIX FALLS, WIS. 54024